For Caleb

A Landen Acres Novel

Natalie Jess

Greenstone Publishing

Cover Design by Storyville Designs

Interior Format by Luna Blooms PA

Edits by My Notes in the Margins

Proofread by My Notes in the Margins

Contents

Dedication

To all my amazing readers – old and new.

Before
For Caleb

While this story can be read on its own, it overlaps the timelines in *For Avery* and *For Sam* where both Matt and Caleb have scenes.

In the bonus chapter of *For Avery*, Jackson, Avery, and Courtney are at the rodeo where Caleb just won, as usual. Caleb is then mentioned in *For Avery* as having participated in the Date a Cowboy auction as the final bachelor. Caleb was the only bachelor to bring in more donations than Jackson.

In *For Sam*, we see Caleb and Matt preparing food in the kitchen, arguing over whether Caleb was cleared by a doctor to ride a bucking horse, and hanging out with the group during and after mudding. Tommy notices a few times where Matt blushes around Caleb or has an odd expression but doesn't say anything. Caleb starts leaving clothes at Landen Acres because he's there so much.

Prologue
Matt

Mid-March

The only sound I register is the beeping of the equipment as I turn the corner with the nurse. I think he's still talking but the foot of Caleb's bed is in view and the panic of the last six hours catches up with me.

Watching the rodeo with my brothers. Seeing Caleb go down. Staring at the screen as he lay there motionless. Talking about who should go visit first once we knew which hospital he was admitted to.

And then the phone call came. The hospital receptionist was calm and kind, but the shock of being Caleb's emergency contact, his *only* emergency contact, had me hauling ass out the door after grabbing a change of clothes and accepting a bag of food Bryant threw together.

His agent, Cooper, isn't on the list. His rodeo buddies aren't on the list. My other brothers aren't on the list. Just me.

"Sir?"

Normally, I'd just laugh at someone calling me *sir*. I'm the youngest brother of five. The baby of the family.

"I'm sorry, what?" I ask the nurse who is handing me a couple of pillows.

"There are blankets in the closet and we're happy to pull the couch flat for you to sleep on if you change your mind." His tone is kind, but I know he's repeating himself.

"Thank you, I'll let you know if I need that, but I don't know that I'll be sleeping." The beeps feel like they're getting louder, reminding me of the room where our dad took his last breath. I need to look at Caleb.

"Okay, we'll need to wake him up soon to check his vitals, do another round of imaging, and get him talking again, but he's pretty banged up so it's a balancing act right now."

"Thank you," I say, again, paying attention to the upcoming procedures. Tucking the pillows under my arm, I pull the notebook Tommy sent with me from my pocket. "What time will that be?"

"Three thirty." Jotting that down, I close the notebook and snap the elastic over the front cover as he continues. "I can bring you some information about his surgery and everything going on if that might be helpful."

"Yes, please." My heart thunders in my chest as the nurse nods, leaving me alone with Caleb.

There's no delaying the inevitable, I suppose. I have to remind myself that they already told me he's going to make it. He's going to recover. The beeps are signs of life, of his strength.

Turning around, my eyes drink in every detail, starting with his right foot, which is bandaged and propped on a few pillows. The blanket isn't covering it and I'm not sure if his toes are cold or if it's off for a reason. Do they need to be able to see it? Is it too tender to even have the weight of a blanket on it?

The footage of the accident starts replaying in my head for the hundredth time, the fall itself in slow motion. The bull twisting in midair as the clock hit seven seconds. A sharp breath empties my lungs, resetting my focus to the present. Without meaning to, I take it all in at once.

My hand covers my mouth as I stare at my best friend laid out on the bed in front of me. One arm is wrapped in a temporary cast up to his shoulder and two of his fingers are in splints. But that's nothing compared to his face. My heart breaks just taking in everything he's been through tonight.

God, at least he seems to be on enough painkillers to sleep. One eye looks like it's likely swollen shut, the skin bright red with cuts littering his entire face. There's a gash on his cheekbone with a clear covering. Six stitches there.

None of us could figure out how his helmet came off. He's never messed around with his safety, but something must have snapped off because it was long gone when he hit the ground.

I can't decide what's harder to see, the brace holding his upper spine in place while they wait for the swelling to go down for more imaging, or the patchy buzzed sections of his hair barely visible under the gauze wrapped around his head. Wires are neatly organized, tracking...who knows what. But his chest rises and falls steadily, his mouth parted as he snores softly.

Finally, I take in the rest of the room. A clear plastic bag with folded, but dirty, clothes. I'd recognize that belt buckle anywhere. Caleb's only sentimental about three things: his truck, his favorite necklace, and that buckle. It's from the first rodeo he won and no matter how many buckles he's earned over the years, this is the one he wears. The *only* one.

Opening the notebook to a clean page, I start a list of things for my brothers to take care of, including stopping by the rodeo to get Caleb's truck and belongings before they move out to their next location next week. The nurse made it clear that Caleb will be here for at least that long and that's only if his injuries are superficial. But according to the doctor's notes, it looks like it'll be longer.

There's a recliner on one side of the bed, away from most of the equipment, so I dump the pillows there and put my bags on the shelves. There's a small bathroom with a shower next to the cupboard where the nurse said I could grab blankets. Leaving them for now, I plunk myself down into the chair, adjusting the pillows, feeling antsy.

Am I supposed to say something to him even if it would wake him up?

God, why was it me? We're close, yes, he's my best friend, but to be the one to help him with his medical decisions?

He's friends with all my brothers, at least to some degree, and while we're the closest, I've never handled talking to an insurance company. I've never had to be there when someone went to the hospital to talk to the doctors or do anything other than say goodbye. What the hell can I do for him?

His hand twitches and he grimaces, but he keeps sleeping. I can't stand to see him in pain so I do what I never do: I hold his hand.

Holding hands just means the person will eventually let go. They'll leave you.

But I weave my fingers through his, careful to avoid the small cuts. Calm washes over me. His calloused hands are warm and allow mine to slip right in, like we've done this before.

"I swear to you I'm not going anywhere." My forehead rests gently on his knuckles. "We're all here for you, but for whatever reason you picked me, know that I'm here and I'm not leaving until you make me. Just be okay."

Those fingers squeeze mine some time later. It's weak for how much strength I know they hold, but my eyes fly open. Damn, I didn't notice I fell asleep. With my face next to our hands. He gives me another squeeze, keeping my hand where it is.

"You came." His voice is gravelly but the sound of it fills me with relief.

"Always," I reply, running my free hand through my hair. "It might be a stupid-ass thing to ask, but how are you?"

Caleb chuckles and immediately winces, closing his eyes for a moment. Grabbing the remote, I press the call button, feeling completely out of my element. I wait for the nurse, not wanting him to talk if it causes pain. His breathing is shallow and strained before he opens his eyes, the one only a little because of the swelling.

The nurse from earlier comes in, pushing a cart of supplies and frowning.

Prologue
Caleb

Pain shoots across my ribcage, radiating through my chest. I *should* care more, but Matthew Landen is holding my hand, giving me butterflies like I'm in middle school.

"Mr. Harlow, can you tell me what changed?" the nurse asks, his voice full of concern while still remaining calm. He checks the screens nearby and the various drips connected to my main IV line.

"It's just my ribs." I wheeze, holding Matt's hand tighter, needing to know he's not a figment of my drugged-up imagination. "I thought laughing might be a good idea."

"It's going to take a bit, but you should be more comfortable in two weeks. But it'll probably be six weeks before they're fully healed. Would you like a boost of pain meds?"

Managing a little nod, the nurse sees my assent and presses a few buttons for the machine to dispense a mini-dose. My thumb barely traces circles on the back of Matt's hand. Waking up to him here, his head next to my good leg and his hand in mine, felt like a dream. But as I watched him, not daring to breathe in case I shattered the illusion, the warmth of his hand bled into mine, and a ragged exhale left his beautiful lips. Lips that I've wanted to kiss for years.

Getting the shit kicked out of me by a bull couldn't take away from the effect he has over me. God, I'm such a sap that I'm almost glad this happened because it means he's here with me.

How fucked up is that?

When all of this is over, I'm going to find a way to tell him. Maybe this is my wake up call to stop doing just-one-more ride, to get my own place and a life away from riding. Haven't I been saying it for years that I was retiring?

Jesus these painkillers are really working. My head is only mildly throbbing and I can barely feel my ribs.

"Cay?" Matt's voice breaks through the fog.

"Hmm?" I ask, opening my eyes and immediately regretting it. When did I close them and when did they turn on every fucking light in this hospital?

"Mr. Harlow, I need to take your blood pressure," the nurse says.

"Okay," I reply, letting my eyes close for a second, my head feeling relief instantly.

"Cay, you have to let go of my hand so he can do that." Matt's voice is soothing as exhaustion weighs me down.

"Right." Reluctantly loosening my grip, Matt untangles our fingers and nothing can replace his warmth.

The nurse wraps the cuff around my arm and it fills until it's uncomfortably tight against my bruised bicep. There's a device on my fingertip and he says something about my blood oxygen levels being good before asking me to open my eyes.

"It's bright," I mumble.

Someone moves around and the lights dim.

"I'm going to check your pupils, Mr. Harlow." A gloved hand lifts my eyelid and a spotlight shines quickly into my eye.

"Fuck," I growl out, weakly swatting him away with my good arm.

"Just one more, sir," the nurse says. He's being gentle with my tender face, but fuck that light is like a knife slicing into my brain. "All done. Would you like something to place over your eyes so the halls aren't so bright as we go for imaging?"

"Please," I say, deflating. It's not his fault. The man is doing his job and making sure this concussion isn't too serious. God I hope I can sleep again after this imaging.

The lights get even dimmer and footsteps approach. These have more of a click than that squeaky sneaker the nurses and doctors have been wearing. A hand, calloused from years of working a family ranch, covers mine.

"Better?" Matt asks.

"Thanks," I reply, flipping my hand over and putting my fingers exactly where they were when I woke up. A sigh escapes me. Why haven't I been doing this for the past year, or three? Jesus, he feels so fucking good. I know exactly how he smells, his spicy cologne with the familiar, distinct scent of horses and leather, but my nose can't pick up a damn thing. There's a good chance I broke it, but it seems like I broke half the bones in my body, so what's one more?

"Did you hear that?" Matt's hand gently jiggles mine. I crack open my good eye, grateful for the lights being so dim. He still looks sleepy, his hair is sticking up all over the place and he must have shaved yesterday because he has a heavy five-o'clock shadow. God, what I wouldn't give to kiss him right now, to feel the scratchiness against my skin...

"We need you to stay awake for the next two hours, then you can sleep a little more, but your pupils are responding sluggishly." The nurse steps into view, distracting me from my little reverie. "Can you do that if we keep things dark?"

I must say something inappropriate because the nurse laughs and Matt blushes, covering his eyes with his free hand. Watching his Adam's apple bob as he clears his throat, my eyes travel down his flannel shirt, knowing what he looks like underneath that fabric. But what I'd love to know is what he's packing in those pants.

"Oh my God, please stop talking," Matt pleads.

I'm feeling light and fairly pain-free, and now a little confused. *Did I say everything I was just thinking?*

"Yes," both men say in unison.

"Whoops," I mumble, realizing I must be giving voice to all my thoughts.

"I can keep him awake," Matt says to the nurse. "Anything other than no screens that I need to keep in mind?"

"No, we want him to be comfortable and to rest. When we're back, we can turn off all the lights except the low ones near the ground. Keep him talking so you know he's awake. Are you coming with us for imaging?"

"Of course, if that's okay."

"Stay with me, please," I whisper.

His hand gives mine a light squeeze. "I won't go anywhere, I promise."

Chapter 1
Matt

Six weeks later

"No, your *other* left, Chuck," Jackson says from the bedroom. There's more grumbling as they get the furniture in place.

"Are you sure I shouldn't go in there? They might kill each other," Tommy mumbles as he passes me groceries to fill the fridge.

"Do you really want to put your life on the line over the placement of Caleb's bed?" He doesn't even crack a smile at that, just grabs a half gallon of milk from a bag and hands it to me before grabbing a pack of Caleb's favorite beer next.

Part of me was hoping he'd stay home today. Being in his ex's apartment building for the first time since she walked out on him was going to be a struggle at best. He was becoming more himself recently, but this seems to remind him how much time he spent just a couple flights of stairs up.

For the umpteenth time, I check my phone. No new messages since Caleb left his physical therapy appointment.

"He's not going to send you a message while he's driving. He'll be safe." I look up at my brother, his tone not judgmental but bland.

"I know. It's just weird that he's driving that far on his own."

The specialists gave him the all-clear to drive last week and he's had me with him for most of his appointments. He's been doing well after each one, just a little tired. But this commute is longer with him officially living in Greenstone so I've been counting down the time the commute should take.

"He'll call us if he needs anything," Tommy says.

Something about that irks me and it shouldn't. Maybe I'm too used to Caleb needing *me*. We had a little bubble where it felt like my best friend and I were taking on the world together, like I was the person he trusted most. The person he chose to be with.

I was also the person he hit on that first night in the hospital.

He was hopped up on pain killers, but he definitely said a few things that made me think something might finally happen between the two of us. I just can't initiate something when he's placed so much trust in me.

God, when he decided to move to Greenstone, I thought he'd finally bring it up, but here we are. I'm organizing his kitchen as my brothers roll out their version of a welcome wagon, and I'm about as sexually frustrated as a guy can be.

But for the first time in my life, I *want* to be with someone. I'm just scared to death for all the ways I could fuck things up.

A thud shakes me out of my weird train of thought as Tommy mumbles something about answering the door. My heart beats faster in anticipation of seeing Caleb.

"What the hell?" Tommy exclaims while holding the door open.

I hear Byant grunt right before one end of a couch seems to float its way into the apartment. A moment later, two beefy arms come into view, and I shouldn't be surprised, especially not at this point in my life, but Bryant is carrying the entire couch by himself.

Once he's inside, Tommy lets the door shut and he races around to grab the far end, trying to take some of the weight.

"Are you trying to get hurt or something?"

Bryant just rolls his eyes and maneuvers everything in front of where the TV's set up.

"Seriously, what are you doing?" Tommy's annoyance is coming through clearly as our older brother gently sets the furniture down with ease.

"It wasn't that heavy," he says, shrugging.

I watch the whole ordeal from the kitchen, knowing better than to poke the bear. If anyone in the family was the embodiment of a damn grizzly, it'd be Bryant, even though he'd never hurt a fly. He just comes off as surly a lot of the time.

"Hey Jax," Chuck sings from the bedroom doorway. "It looks like we don't have to get the couch."

"What do you mean—" Jax comes into the living room and shuts his mouth. I can see his fist clenching from over here, something he always does when stressed. "God damn it, you can't go around hauling shit like that yourself."

Bryant's arms cross over his chest and he raises an eyebrow. "And why not?"

The other two join me in the kitchen, none of us wanting to piss them off further. I smack Chuck on the back of his head and mouth, "What were you thinking?"

He just chews his toothpick with abandon and whispers, "Oops," back to me.

"Because you can't get hurt." Jackson runs a hand down his face in exasperation.

"Why would I? It wasn't heavy."

"It's not light. It was stupid of you to haul a fucking couch from the moving van into the apartment on your own."

"So now I'm stupid?" Bryant's deep voice is almost amused as he looks down at our oldest brother, not an easy feat to accomplish for most people.

"No. But you could have thrown out your damn back, and then where would we be?"

"Only one man down. We have people who can cover."

"And they're already covering for Matt." As soon as it slips out, everyone's staring at me.

Fuck, it feels like when Dad died and they didn't know where I'd live because I was a minor—everyone watching me and talking about me, just never talking *to* me.

"I'm still getting most of my work done," I say defensively, guilt filling me because they've needed to find ways to make sure nothing gets dropped.

"I know and you don't need to be. You're taking care of Caleb, and we have things covered," Jax says. "All I'm saying is we can't risk an injury over something that could easily be avoided."

"Can you all just trust me to know my own limits?"

"Bryant, you know that's not what I meant."

"Whatever, it's fine." The way he says it sounds anything but. He checks his phone. "I need to head out soon."

"Got a hot date?" Chuck asks.

Another eye roll. "No, I told you all the other day that Gerald has an appointment this afternoon."

"You sure Dr. Thompson takes pets that are half wolf?"

"I checked with them and they're okay with it."

They keep talking while my attention is pulled back to the door, feeling an invisible tug. A moment later, the knob turns and Caleb walks in almost silently. He looks worn out but good. His gaze finds mine almost immediately and he grins at me, making my knees oddly weak. My face feels hot all of a sudden and I'm blushing.

If I don't get my reactions under control, my brothers will give me so much shit for finally having feelings for someone.

Chapter 2
Caleb

My first thought upon seeing Matt blushing in my new kitchen when I open the door is *God, I'd love to come home to this every day.*

Hell, I'd even take his arguing brothers.

Then reality sinks in that Matt's my best friend and he's the first one to tell me what a piece of shit boyfriend he is. He's never cheated or anything, he's just never been able to let someone in. Plus, I think he's only ever been with women, so he might be incredibly uncomfortable if his best friend said he had feelings for him.

I must be a masochist for even letting the idea of trying to be with him bounce around in my brain again. Granted, I've been riding bulls and broncos for a living for the past ten years after getting out from under my father's thumb, so most people might not consider me the most practical person.

By the time my boots are off, Matt is at my side, taking the bag with my change of clothes. Call me stubborn, but it feels so much more normal to drive my truck wearing my jeans, flannel, and boots. I bring my sneakers and sweats to my physical therapy appointments and change in the bathroom before we begin. Lord knows I need to feel normal as much as possible these days.

"How'd it go?" I can see Matt looking me over for any signs that something is wrong, but instead of being annoyed, all I can think about is how damn good he smells. Just like horses with a hint of leather. "Cay?"

Shit, I must have been staring at him too long. "It went well. I had someone new today, but they were cool."

"Good. And the drive?" His gaze scrutinizes my features like he thinks I might have overdone something.

"I wore my sunglasses the whole time and didn't have the radio on, so I focused like a fucking champ."

"Good," he repeats and then he laughs a little in relief, smiling enough for some of his freckles to disappear as he pats me on the back. "You should go lay down, Chuck and Jax have your bed set up already."

And my good mood turns sour.

I know that I need to rest. My brain needs it. But for fuck's sake I'm so damn sick of it.

It's not until now that I realize the arguing between Jax and Bryant stopped and everyone is watching me. They look happy that I'm back but also a little worried.

Everyone is always worried.

Clearing my throat, I decide to not act like a petulant child and argue that I don't need a nap. Instead, I harness some of that charm from a decade on the circuit schmoozing with fans and sponsors. "That sounds like what the doctor ordered. But first, I want to see everything you've done with the place. It's looking like a real home, guys."

"If you missed the first part of the argument, Bryant is responsible for the couch being here," Chuck says from the kitchen, much to Tommy's dismay who backhands him in the chest.

"As long as no one got hurt," I say, looking at Bryant and Jax with sympathy, "then I'm thrilled it's here, however it was carried."

"Smooth," Matt murmurs. He's close enough that I feel the barest hint of his breath, which sends a shiver down my spine. Then he tips his head towards the living room. "Let's give you a quick tour and I can show you the kitchen set-up after you rest."

Things look fantastic and I do my best to not feel guilty that they did the literal heavy lifting. I remind myself that I've already talked to the Landens about helping out on their ranch now that I'm living nearby and this isn't just them giving me their time and energy. It'll be reciprocated and maybe I'll find a place there long-term. Invest in the ranch's future.

They really have done a great job in a short amount of time. The living room looks better than it did at my old place, and Tommy is making sure all of my accounts are synced for streaming services on my TV. The table is set up next to the kitchen and a few of my awards are on the walls. My dressers, side tables, bed, and even my new blackout curtains are set up.

"Did Chuck get me a throw pillow?" I ask Matt as I laugh and stare at a square pillow that reads *save a horse, ride a cowboy.*

"Damn it, Chuck," he calls out the bedroom door. "You promised no funny business."

Chuck saunters in, a cocky grin on his face. "There's nothing funny about it. It's a serious message that will set the mood for Caleb's visitors."

Matt looks slightly mortified and speechless. "He's not... I mean, he hasn't been..."

The poor guy seems flustered.

"Actually, I was just cleared for riding today," I say, trying to help out Matt. "Nothing too crazy, of course. Maybe I'll add a sticky note so it reads *save a horse,* gently *ride a cowboy.*"

Chuck cackles and slaps me on the back before leaving the room while Matt blinks and looks me over. It must be my imagination that his gaze lingers on my crotch. But damn, if he wanted to ride me, I'd be his stallion in a heartbeat.

"You should sleep," Matt says after clearing his throat and closing the curtains. It becomes very apparent to me that we're alone in my bedroom. "We'll keep it quiet out there as we bring in the final pieces of furniture."

Any thoughts of him finally coming on to me with a clear signal he wants this flee my head. His brothers are still here.

Not that something was going to happen anyway.

Grudgingly, I grab a pair of athletic shorts to sleep in.

"Do you have everything you need?" he asks, pausing in the doorway.

"To take a nap?"

"Well, yeah, it's a new space and all." He rubs the back of his neck and seems to look everywhere except my bed.

"Do you think anything is missing?" I ask, shrugging. "No?"

He seems weirdly out of his element. It's not like he hasn't physically tucked me into bed since the accident, so I don't know why he's being so odd now.

"Then I'm sure everything's in place."

He nods and turns to leave, pulling at the doorknob to likely return to the kitchen.

"Matt?"

"Yeah?" A hopeful look crosses his face but I'm not sure for what.

"Everything really looks amazing, thanks."

A small smile creeps across his face. "It was nothing. Get some rest, and when you're awake I'll spend way too much time telling you all about how I organized your pantry."

Then he has the audacity to wink and shut the door, leaving me temporarily speechless.

Who knew kitchen organization could be such a turn-on?

Chapter 3
Matt

The door closes with a soft *click*, shutting me off from the rodeo star I'm lusting after harder and harder the more I'm around him.

Maybe he's an ex-rodeo star now?

Former? That seems better. The former rodeo star. Or maybe that sounds like he's washed up and trying too hard.

"Oh my god," I grumble quietly to myself.

Judging by the way people react to seeing him in public, he's still very much a star, he's just not riding bulls and broncos like he was born on one.

I shake my head and walk to the couch where Tommy has the latest round of medical bills laid out. Because he's better with organizing information and numbers, Caleb agreed to let him handle these. When I saw the first few come through, I called my brother right away, feeling completely out of my element and like I might screw up something with his insurance.

"Everything good?"

"Yeah, I'm just double checking I'm not missing anything." He looks up, shuffling a paper to the back of one of his piles. "How's he feeling?"

"Okay, it seems," I say, shrugging. "I'm guessing he won't sleep long, if at all, with us here."

He types something into the site he's on, glancing back at the top paper every few strokes. "I'm just about done with this and can help some more, just tell me what else needs to happen."

"I think it's just the final few loads of chairs and lamps."

"Okay, then we might head out in a few minutes, if you think it's okay with Caleb."

"You're welcome to stay longer, you know."

Tommy smirks. "If Jax and I stay after Bryant leaves, you know Chuck will want to as well. He looks worn out and doesn't need to entertain four cowboys."

Oh shit. There's that flutter in my gut that happens whenever I know it's going to be just the two of us. I try to will it away because it's not like anything is going to magically happen today after the hours, days, and weeks we've already been alone together.

"True," I say as normally as possible while willing my cheeks to not redden. I stand abruptly to reset my mind and not think of all the ways I'd like to wake up Caleb right now. "I'll go haul whatever's left."

I need to get my head on right.

After a full thirty minutes, I finally hear signs of movement coming from the bedroom. Not wanting to stare at the door, I grab a magazine from the coffee table and open to a random story just to give me something to do—or appear like I have something to do.

There's a very good chance I'm glossing over the same paragraph again and again without reading a single word. At least my brothers left so I'm not being teased for glancing at the bedroom door every fifteen seconds.

Finally, the doorknob turns and Caleb is leaving his still-darkened bedroom. He's still wearing those red athletic shorts that hang loose on his thighs, but mold perfectly to his ass, and it's hard to not stare as I close the magazine.

"Are you feeling okay?"

That question earns me a light-hearted eye roll. "Yes, it was good that I took a nap."

One hand scratches his belly, which lifts the hem of his shirt, and I catch a glimpse of the line of dark hair leading down into his shorts.

Get it together.

I put the magazine back on the coffee table and, as casually as I can manage, I cross my legs to hide my growing erection. It's not like he has to try hard to get my attention, especially not when his voice is gruff from sleep and his curls are messed up, sticking every which way.

Practically begging my hands to run through them.

He walks to the couch and plunks down in his usual spot with a smile. "You guys left the cushions in the same places."

"Yep," I say, leaving out the detail that I put them in the correct spots the moment my brothers left. They had put Caleb's cushion upside down and on the wrong end.

"What'd you read?" He tips his chin towards the magazine.

Shit, I didn't think he'd ask me about it and I try not to squirm. Unsurprisingly, he subscribes to publications about rodeos. This issue has someone riding a stallion on the cover. "I was just flipping through to see if something caught my eye."

He looks at me expectantly.

"I was turning to the feature when you came out, so I didn't read much."

There's always a feature story, right? God, when was the last time I picked up a print magazine?

"It's a good one, you'd probably like it." He tosses an arm over the back of the couch casually and it makes me wonder what it might feel like to be tucked against him. It's a bizarre thought.

I'm not a cuddler. My therapist used to say my need to keep certain intimate acts at arm's length, like holding hands, snuggling, having someone else's arm around me, had to do with our mom leaving after being the primary person to show love with physical affection. She was always there with a hug or her hand ready to take mine.

Well, that was before abandoning us. It's odd that I'm even curious about how it would feel with Caleb when my exes asked for it and I always had an excuse to avoid it.

"Matt?"

"Sorry, what'd you say?" I shake my head to clear my thoughts from the odd path they took.

"I was just talking a little about the story, but your mind seemed to go somewhere else."

There's a pause. He didn't ask a question, but one hangs in the air. He does this every now and then when he notices something takes me out of the moment, but he doesn't push me to share. He gives me space to talk if I want.

Maybe one day I will.

If I do, he'd be the easiest to talk to. He had his own shitty upbringing even if he wasn't here, like my brothers and me. We were all hurt by her, but they cut ties long before I did. I don't know why it took me until I was fifteen. Maybe it was because I was too young to remember everything else? She seemed happy to me and then one day, her bags were packed.

Her wanting me to move out to the coast after Dad died really fucked with me.

Shit, I'm in my head again.

"Sorry," I say, rubbing my hands on my thighs and grounding myself.

"Don't apologize. I'm here if you want to talk."

He watches me as he remains calm and steady, never looking bored or frustrated even though I should be the one making sure he's okay.

"Thanks. Just remembering something, no big deal."

"Alright. Are you up for a game?" he asks, gesturing to the system Tommy set up.

"Only if you're wearing your blue light glasses."

"Yes, nurse Landen," he grumbles. Before he can get up, I stop him with a hand on his chest, feeling the warmth of his skin through the soft, white fabric. I must be imagining things because I think he takes a sharp breath before I remove my hand.

My throat feels thick with need, and I clear it as I quickly stand in hopes that he won't hear how badly he's affected me in less than two minutes. "I'll get them. You pick what we play."

A moment alone should help me clear my head, but as I enter the bedroom, I groan because all I can smell is *him*.

"He's your best friend, damn it," I remind myself under my breath. "That's what he needs. Not another person wanting to get in his pants."

The pillow Chuck got him grabs my attention. It's completely unreasonable, but I feel like it's mocking me. Once I've gotten the glasses from the bedside table, I can't seem to stop myself from flipping it over so I can't read the text anymore.

Not that he needs a reminder for sex. Now that they've cleared him for more vigorous activities, I'll just have another thing to try to keep my mind off of.

Great.

Chapter 4
Caleb

It's weird how this place feels more like a home than my last apartment did and I haven't even spent the night here yet.

Maybe it has something to do with knowing I'm not traveling constantly.

Maybe it's because I finally chose a town with people I want to be near.

For the first time in a decade, my life doesn't revolve around the rodeo circuit.

I glance over at the person who brought me here. He's concentrating on the screen while he finishes up the race. It's been fairly slow, but the stress that built up for him after my accident seems to be leaving him. It was ever present the first two weeks where any new beep or alert on my equipment sent his shoulders up to his ears.

I'd try to ask him how he was doing or if he needed a break. We finally got into a rhythm where I'd ask if he was okay, he'd grunt a mono-syllabic response about being fine, and then I'd call him a liar, and he'd crack a smile.

The smile that always makes my pulse increase. But being hooked up to medical equipment meant I'd always try to keep him talking so he wouldn't see how much he affected me.

Maybe it would've put me out of my misery if he had figured it out then.

I sometimes wonder just how bad it would be if I said something. But then my stomach sours at the thought of him rejecting me and growing distant. Or worse, thinking that our friendship was just me trying to get into his pants and losing him that way.

Who knows...he could be harboring secret feelings for me, too. *Doubtful.*

I've definitely caught him looking at me every now and then, and there was the night he held my hand, but he seems to pull back or clear his throat to reset himself whenever it feels like we're having a moment.

"Those glasses seem to be doing something since you thoroughly kicked my ass that time," he says, chuckling.

Damn, that's a sexy sound.

"They're still annoying but you were right that I should get them. I think I'm getting back to my old self already. I really sucked the first few times we played after—" The rest of the sentence dies on my tongue. Even though the accident still seems to dictate every moment of my life, it's hard to bring it up at times.

"Yeah, you are getting back to your old self." He sets down his controller and gestures towards the kitchen. "I think it might be time for your tour."

"And maybe a snack," I add as we both get up and I put my glasses on the coffee table while resisting a sigh. Maybe someday I'll stop thinking of how much I'd like to have *him* for a snack.

The sleeves of his flannel shirt are rolled up to just below his elbows, showing off toned forearms and strong hands that are used to manual labor. But I've seen some of the more delicate things he's created when he cooks, too. There's a strength to his gentleness that most people don't get to see. A softness behind an exterior that isn't unfriendly but can be hard to read if you don't know him.

"Let's start with your pantry," he says, opening the door and revealing neatly stocked shelves. "We threw out most of the stuff from your old place because half of it was close to expiring so you have new staples. I think we got everything except one or two ramen flavors that weren't in stock."

I nod, focusing on what he's pointing to on the shelves and not the ways the muscles of his forearm shift with each motion.

"Your spice selection was pretty atrocious, as you well know, so I took the liberty of getting you a few blends that work well for things like chicken, beef, and fish, and then Italian seasonings so you have more variety than generic barbecue and Tex-Mex." He gives me some serious side-eye.

Really, he's been giving me grief for my eating habits since the accident because he had to stop by my old place often while I was hospitalized. If he didn't seem to be having so much fun at my expense, I would probably be annoyed, but I love that he notices small things like this.

"I happen to know what I like," I say.

"And it's okay to branch out a little every now and then," he counters. "Or at least have decent options for when I cook here."

Oh, I like the idea of him cooking here regularly far too much and need to get my mind on a different train of thought. "Like you wouldn't just bring your own spices from the ranch."

"That's irrelevant."

"So, when am I cooking an Italian meal from scratch where I'll be needing the spices versus using my favorite jar of marinara?" I can't help but needle him just a little.

"I don't know," he says, shrugging. "Maybe you'll want to impress someone before they see your special pillow."

Is that a little jealousy I hear?

"You mean all the dates trying to bang down my door as we speak?"

"I don't know," he repeats and lets out a breath. "At some point you'll bring someone back here and you might want to talk before..."

"Bringing out the pillow?" I offer, wanting badly to tell him the only person I'm interested in is already in my apartment.

Damn, maybe I need to start socializing again.

"Yeah, before bringing out the pillow." He rolls his eyes before going back to the tour for another five minutes.

"Want to grab a drink at Maybel's?" I practically blurt.

There's a pause while a frown appears on his too-handsome-for-his-own-good face. He freezes in his crouch with one hand on a jar he's filled with flour nestled with other baking supplies in a low drawer. I wait, giving him the time he needs to gather his thoughts.

"I don't think that's a good idea."

Well shit. That idea backfired beautifully and now I'm afraid I've fucked things up between us before even getting a chance to see if this isn't one-sided.

"Um, yeah, that's fine. Forget I said anything."

"That's not what I meant," he says, backtracking. "I meant it's not a good idea for you to add another big thing to your day. You had physical therapy. You drove yourself. You're in a new apartment, which is another level of overstimulation. I'd just think adding the sights and sounds of a bar could really wipe you out."

"I didn't say today," I say, a small smirk appearing unbidden knowing he wasn't shutting me down completely.

"We could go tomorrow evening?" he offers. "But you'll need to have your earplugs to dampen the sound so you don't get overwhelmed."

"I can do that."

Getting a beer sounds pretty great right about now. The whole thing might help me loosen up and get my mind off how much I'd like to be more than friends with the man in front of me.

Chapter 5
Matt

This is a terrible idea.

I feel like I signed on to be Caleb's wingman, even though he didn't even hint at that being his plan this evening.

He put his earplugs in on the short ride from his apartment to the bar and immediately talked way too loud. By the time he's speaking at a regular volume, we're already parking.

For the tenth time this trip, I stop myself from asking if he's still feeling up for this. God, I just hate seeing him overwhelmed from his TBI.

"Shit," he murmurs, digging in his pocket for his phone and answering it with a tentative, "Hello?"

It's a woman's voice on the other end, but I can't hear anything she says.

"Yeah, call me Caleb. Who is this?" He pulls his phone away from his ear and puts the conversation on speaker.

"Sorry to interrupt your evening. This is Samantha Jones, you can call me Sam. I work for the town of Greenstone, and I got your number from my friend Jackson Landen. I hope you don't mind my phoning."

I hold back a snicker. *Friend*, my ass. They were showing up to functions together for a full month after she moved to town. Jax never brings anyone anywhere as a date and hooks up with whoever he wants. They were definitely hooking up regularly.

My oldest brother has one friend and that's Chase Barnett, not the new PR person for Greenstone.

"Not at all, Jax is a friend. What can I do for you, Sam?" he asks.

"I'll be brief and I'm happy to send along all the details, but we're organizing a fundraiser for new veterinary equipment to attract a new large animal veterinarian for the area. The main attraction, so to speak, is a dating auction with the theme 'Date A Cowboy' where people bid in a live auction to go on a group date with one of the bachelors. Jacksy mentioned that you were moving to town and might be available."

"When is this?"

"In May, so it's only a month's notice, I'm sorry."

I pull out my phone and jot down the details for him.

"And, uh, do I get to keep my clothes on?"

If I had been eating, I would have choked. Instead my mouth hangs open and I stare at the man sitting next to me and try desperately not to picture him stripping.

"Pardon?" Sam says, just as stunned as me.

"How do I put this delicately..." he says, pausing. "Is this a family-friendly event where the bachelors stay dressed?"

"Oh goodness, I see what you're asking now. Absolutely fully clothed participants for the entire event."

"Okay, thanks for clarifying." He sounds completely casual right now, while I'm still in shock. "I can text you my info and if you send me the rest of the details, I'll give you a definitive answer before the end of tomorrow, but it sounds like something I'd like to participate in or help with in some way."

"Wonderful, thank you so much," she exclaims. "I'll get everything ready to send your way shortly."

They hang up and I still haven't moved. He hasn't looked at me, either.

"You seem to have short-circuited," he observes.

"Beyond the date for the event, your only question was if you get to keep your clothes on."

"Are you asking me something?"

Now he's looking right at me and I feel like squirming under his gaze. I have no problem with people taking off their clothes for work. And I'd like to pretend that the guy I can't get out of my head stripping for anyone other than me wouldn't make me a little jealous. Mostly because he has no reason to consider my feelings about who he'd be going home with.

Fuck me. My head is a complete shitshow right now and he's waiting for me to say something.

Anything.

Jesus, I'm still not talking.

At this point, what could I even say that wasn't ridiculous?

Thankfully, he clears his throat and breaks the tension.

"It's something I learned to ask years ago," he explains while putting his earplug back in. "My first agent asked once while I was only half-listening but it got my full attention. He was arranging for me to join a group event at a private function, and it hadn't crossed my mind as something to check, but ever since then, I want to make sure that expectations are clear for anything I may do."

"Yeah, you wouldn't want to be surprised, I suppose."

His chuckle breaks some of the tension I'm feeling. "No, that would be less than ideal."

"Have you ever done anything you weren't comfortable with?" I ask, truly curious because though we've become better friends, there's still a lot I don't know about his early years in the rodeo and even the family he left a decade ago.

"Not like that, no. But I've needed to talk to groups of people or individuals to try to win them over for a sponsorship or something else, and I always felt out of place." He looks out his windows to the mountains for a moment. "I have financial security now, but it wasn't always like that and, well, I stay on bulls and broncos for a living. Stayed, I guess. Schmoozing with rich city folk who've never sat in a saddle took a while to get used to."

"You do great with crowds," I point out.

"They're all a blur for the most part. Plus, that's competition time, so it was always easy to feed off their energy." He glances at the entrance. "Time for that beer?"

I half-forgot we're sitting in the parking lot of a bar.

"Yeah, let's go in."

Maybe a drink will do me some good.

Chapter 6
Caleb

Even with the lot being partially full, it still feels busy inside Maybel's. I've only been here once a few years ago when I was near Greenstone for a competition and I met up with Matt and Chuck. Come to think of it, it was long enough ago that Matt couldn't even order liquor. Chuck danced up a storm and talked us into joining with a handful of locals I can't remember for the life of me.

But it was a good night, one that made me want to see these guys more.

To find a place to settle with people I care about, rather than picking a town that's close to where I train.

Trained.

Even after two months, it's odd to think of bull riding as my past. I'm not too many years from when I assumed I'd need to retire, but the sudden nature of how it all ended throws me off.

A hand presses into my lower back and without turning around, I know it's Matt's. My eyes drift closed as I relish the sensation of his touch, if only for a moment.

"How about a table in the corner where it's a little quieter for tonight?" The brim of his hat bumps against mine and even though his voice is muted, I'm hyper-aware of each word.

Glancing at the bar, which has a handful of people leaning against the counter already, and then to the small dance floor, a table in the corner does seem like the best bet for tonight. I nod and feel his fingers add a little pressure, guiding me in the direction of the table he'd like.

Of course they're gone a second later.

It's not like we're on a date.

"Caleb Harlow?" a voice asks as a new hand touches my bicep. Years of practice keeps me from pulling my arm out of the stranger's reach. This is especially jarring since my mind is trying to memorize the warmth that was just at my back.

I put a smile on my face and turn to look at the woman who is watching me, starstruck, as her hand drops to her side.

"Yes, ma'am," I say, touching the brim of my hat.

"Oh my goodness, I can't believe you're here! I'm a huge fan," she says, her voice extra quiet, but I can still make out what she's saying. A blush appears on her cheeks as she shakes her blonde curls back and forth in excitement.

"It's always great to meet a fan. What's your name?" I ask, knowing the likelihood of me remembering it is much lower than it was before the accident.

"I'm Candace. What are you in town for?"

"Actually, I just moved here." There's no use in hiding it, I suppose. I'm guessing Cooper would have liked me to make an official announcement or at least a small press release, but I asked to keep things quiet while I focused on my rehab. "Greenstone always seemed like a nice place to retire, don't you think?"

That's the first time I've used the word "retire" outside of talking to the Landens and my recovery team. Maybe it should feel weird, but I might be more ready for it than I imagined I would be.

She looks a little surprised. "Well, it's not exactly a destination for most people, but you'd be hard pressed to find a better community."

"Exactly what I'm hoping for." I glance around to find Matt sitting at a table, checking over the menu with a cranky look on his face. "I should head over, but it was lovely to meet you."

Damn it, I already forgot her name.

She doesn't seem to notice though as she thanks me for chatting and goes back to her friend at the bar.

When I reach our table, bright blue eyes sneak a quick look at me over the top of the menu that's supposed to be absorbing his attention. I almost say something about his now-sullen mood, but I don't know how to navigate this. Usually, if one of us pisses off the other, which rarely happens, we just spit it out, get it off our chests, and move on. Or it's obvious what happened.

I've hung out with Matt plenty of times with fans stopping by to introduce themselves and he's never bothered by it. So I can't figure out what happened in the last minute that would make him cranky.

"What do you want?" I ask instead, nodding at his menu while I pick up mine. It's odd to be getting a drink in public after so long, but it feels good.

Normal.

"Probably a cider and their loaded fries." He's trying to sound like nothing is wrong but even with earplugs in, I can hear the strain. "What about you?"

"A beer and some sort of appetizer. I don't remember what we had last time."

"I think we had several rounds of shots before beers thanks to Chuck." He cracks a smile and some of the tension leaves him.

"That sounds about right."

"Why don't we split a few so you can see what you like, it's been a while since you were last here."

I nod, liking that idea a lot.

A man approaches our table with a pad and pen.

"Hey Kieth," Matt says. "How's your mom feeling?"

"Grateful to be out of her cast, that's for sure. She sends her thanks for the latest delivery."

Matt waves him off. "Not necessary, you know that. Just happy to help a little."

The server must have noticed my confusion because he says, "Matt's been making homemade soups and sauces for a few years now and donating them to the local food shelf that my mom runs. Well, it's less of a place and more of a delivery service where people can sign up for what they need."

"You always made it sound like your 'extras' were for neighbors."

He blushes. "I try to do a few batches each month, it's not a big deal."

"It sounds like a big deal to those who get what they need because of you."

"And whatever he makes is always some of the first things to go," Kieth adds.

"That's not surprising," I say, thinking about the meals Matt brought me over the past month. Every dish was great.

It's not a secret he likes to cook, but he already balances a lot with his responsibilities at the ranch. Add in all the time he's been spending with me and I'm not sure when he found the time to cook for the food shelf, but he must have.

It makes me feel guilty for all the time I've taken up the last several weeks.

I'd also like to help without him feeling like I'm stepping in on his *thing*. Maybe for now I can quietly donate some money while I figure it all out.

Chapter 7
Matt

We order and I'm sure my cheeks are pink from all the attention on what I do for the community. I know it's a big deal for the food shelf to be able to offer homemade soup and sauce made from local farmers and ranchers, but I'm not used to hearing about it in front of anyone who isn't one of my brothers.

Two thoughts war inside of me.

First, I picture what it might be like if Caleb were by my side while I cook. All the ways we might bump into each other, or scenarios where our hands might touch...

The second thought fighting for dominance is seeing Candy approach him. His cool confidence in chatting with her reminded me that this man can have pretty much anyone he wants. Even if someone didn't know anything about bull riding, he's still drop-dead gorgeous. So whether it's his celebrity status, or just his charm and good looks, he has hundreds of options that are so much better than me.

If he's even looking right now.

Would he hook up with someone I used to see?

He might feel guilty if he found out after the fact, or be mad at me for not telling him since I obviously saw them talking.

"Matthew?"

Shit, he usually only uses that name after he's tried to get my attention a few times.

"I know Candy," I say without preamble.

He looks at me, confused.

"You know, Candy." I subtly cock my head towards the bar. "We used to hook up, but it was never serious."

"Who are you talking about?" He still seems lost.

"You were talking to her a few minutes ago," I explain.

"Oh, her," he replies, realization dawning on him. "She said her name right away and I couldn't remember it for anything."

"She might have said Candace?" I offer, hating to see the frustration he tries to hide over how hard it is to remember a new person's name since his accident.

I make a mental note to try to use people's names around him so he has a better chance at remembering.

A moment later, our drinks come, and I thank Kieth by name before he leaves us alone again. I'm grateful for my cold cider to wash down some of the awkwardness I'm feeling.

"Is there a particular reason you told me about hooking up with Candy?" The confidence he so recently displayed seems to have drained away as he picks at the napkin under his beer.

"It's a small town and I didn't want you to find out later and be mad I didn't say something."

"What now?"

I bite back a groan of frustration, swallowing the jealousy at the thought of something happening, and get the words out for my best friend. "I never dated her but wanted you to be aware that she and I hooked up a few times over the years. There aren't any lingering feelings or anything."

"And you want me to know this in case I...want something from her?"

A few sips later and I feel a little more comfortable with this conversation and just being there for him. "Yeah, you're cleared for a lot of activities now and might be looking for something. She was definitely starstruck and could be interested."

"What makes you think I'd be interested in her?" He's studying me, like he's trying to read into my responses. Honestly, he let me off the hook when he sat down because I know he could see I was upset.

"I suppose we haven't done too much together with dates around."

"I don't think I've ever seen you with the same person more than once," he counters.

"That's probably true," I admit. "It's a topic my therapist and I talked about quite a bit back in the day."

"How so?" He shifts so he's leaning forward, forearms resting against the table, his napkin forgotten for now.

"I had a pattern that became pretty noticeable by the time college started when I began working with her. It wasn't anything I had consciously tried to do, but I had only been dating people who recently moved to Greenstone. Never anyone who knew me, or who had known me before my dad passed. I mean, the pattern started before then, but my 'relationships' got shorter and shorter and only with new-to-town women."

"What was wrong with someone knowing you?" Concern shines in his eyes as he searches my face like he might find the explanation there.

"The more someone knows you, and the more you know them, the more hurt you'll be when it's over." It feels weird to say that out loud, even to my best friend. I've only ever talked with Mary about the *why*.

"Everyone's afraid of getting hurt," he says gently.

"Oh, I know. There's just only so much a person can take after he's been left." Now I'm not just talking about dating.

I was the straw that broke the camel's back and made our mother leave Greenstone and move to the coast. Sure, I was only five when it happened, but I remember how she'd hold my hands one minute and then I'd hear her arguing with Dad over how badly she needed to go. When he died, she messaged me with some half-assed offer that I could come live with her, reminding me she was my guardian. It was laughable how little she tried to be there for me even when I was completely untethered and scared shitless while also mourning the loss of the man who raised me.

Cay studies me for a bit. Maybe waiting for me to elaborate. Possibly thinking it's pretty odd that I haven't dated anyone who knows me well. I've never had that someone to connect with who I don't keep secrets from.

But because it's Caleb sitting across from me, I feel the urge to give him a little more. It might be stupid and meaningless to him, but nothing with this man feels stupid or meaningless to me.

"It's always been easier to connect physically with someone than emotionally. And you can only be with someone for so long before they start needing more from you. Pursuing someone who knew little-to-nothing about me and was also distracted by getting to know where they fit in Greenstone bought me more time before needing to pull away."

Chapter 8
Caleb

My heart breaks a little hearing his confession. It's no secret that he's never been in a long-term relationship. The few times he brought a date to the rodeo it was never the same girl. Whenever he'd mention dating someone, it wasn't ever more than a handful of months before he'd say things just weren't quite right and didn't work out.

"It's been a bit since you've dated anyone. Are you still feeling the same way?" The words come out casual, like there isn't a mountain of hope precariously in the balance in his answer.

"You mean am I still trying to avoid dating someone who knows me?"

I nod.

"Damn, I'd like to say that I'm not," he says, letting out a long breath that turns into a chuckle. "But I'm scared shitless to try most of the time. Dating someone who knows me, or who I'd open up to so they *could* know me, means that I can lose someone else. I know it sounds stupid, trust me. When I say it out loud I can hear it."

"It's not stupid." I want to reach across the table and cover his hand with mine. To show him that he *can* have it all with someone who knows him.

"Maybe not, but the little voice in my head reminds me that I'm not enough."

I wait for him to explain, but he takes a drink and shrugs.

"Not enough for what?"

"Anyone." He says it nonchalantly and my heart really breaks now.

Because part of him believes it.

He believes that he's not enough of a reason for someone to stay.

"That's not true."

"Logically, I know that, but history has shown me something else, so I'm working on it."

I want to ask him what that means. I know the basics about his parents, so I understand that. My thoughts go to him *working on it* by dating and my stomach sours.

God, I wish I could show him how wrong that little voice is. If I could make him see how he's more than enough to stay for...I'd jump at the chance.

"So, the nice woman who introduced herself to me—"

"Candy or Candace," he interjects, which helps me remember a little better.

"—wasn't someone who knew you well?" I ask.

"We both grew up here, but I think she was one of the exceptions since we were pretty open about not wanting to date."

Even though I'm jealous, it feels good to have Matt opening up like this. Instead of just updates about changes in our relationships, we can talk about what works and what doesn't. All I want is for him to be happy, so I can swallow my pride that wants to poke and prod him until I get a clear answer about how he feels, or doesn't feel, about me. I can be that friend.

"Maybe the person you should try dating is standing over by the bar. She seemed nice."

There's a split second where I see a wince and then Matt clears his expression. "I appreciate the nudge, but she's not someone I'm interested in."

"Another Greenstone gal?" I can hear how ridiculous I sound asking that. But something in me just needs to know if there's someone he has his eye on.

"Ah no," he says, his hand leaving his cider and rubbing the back of his neck like he's uncomfortable about something. "No Greenstone *gal*."

The emphasis he puts on the word catches my attention. Matt has only ever spoken of being with women or being attracted to them. I've been secretly hoping I might have a chance and now my heart rate seems to have doubled.

I swallow hard. "Does that mean there's someone who has your attention who isn't one?"

A light pink spreads over his cheeks. "You could say that, yes."

Well shit. Is he talking about the person not being from Greenstone or not being a woman? Does it matter? It either means the person he's interested in isn't a woman or doesn't live here.

If we were having this conversation a month ago—before we started coordinating my move—I would have held out hope that it was me. I'd have fit the bill.

Before I can open my mouth to ask another question, plates of food are placed on our table and we're chatting with the server. Thankfully, Matt greets him by name again and I repeat it a few more times in my head, hoping it'll stick.

The food is pretty good and the conversation is easy, but we don't feel the need to fill every second with chatter. It's one of the things that drew me to Matt years ago as a friend. We seem to understand a lot about each other.

Just not *everything*, which is okay.

This simply isn't a date, nor will there be one in the future. I'd rather grab drinks and dinner with my best friend than fuck that up.

I take out my earplugs when we're back in his truck and everything feels extra loud for a moment as I get used to the change. It's something easy to focus on rather than breathing in the familiar and comforting smells in this small space.

Matt's quiet for most of the short drive, his grip on the steering wheel tightening every now and then. I glance over at him a few times and he seems to be mulling something over, so I wait, giving him the space to choose his words if he needs to.

Finally, he puts the truck in park and turns to face me.

"I'm not only attracted to women," he blurts out, looking right at me for a moment before picking at a loose thread on his jeans. "I just wanted to be clear about that, even though I haven't dated any guys."

Hope that this is it, that this is when he tells me this isn't one-sided, fills me to the brim.

But nothing else comes.

He's opening up about his sexuality because he's only told me about the women he's been with. Because we're friends who support each other and talk about who they're dating.

So before I leave, I force myself to smile and say, "Thanks for telling me, that will help me be a better wingman for you when we go out next."

He picks at that thread a little longer before finally looking up. "Yeah, sure."

I'm about to ask him if something is wrong when he asks if I'd like help with anything. Now I feel like I was crossing my fingers that my caretaker likes me, so I reassure him that I'm good and will get to sleep shortly.

But when I'm in my apartment a minute later, I'm surrounded by reminders of the person who doesn't feel the same way. Instead of falling asleep, I lie in bed, staring at my ceiling for a few hours just giving myself one night to imagine what life could have been if he felt differently.

Chapter 9
Matt

One month later

Instead of going to the first-ever Date a Cowboy Auction where two of my brothers are helping bring in donations, I'm turning off the small highway to go to the park feeling like a coward. Smoke from our cousin Jesse's barbecue is rising from just around the hillside where the post-auction group dinner will be hosted.

Post-auction group *date*.

My jaw clenches. Why am I still so agitated about this? A little voice in the back of my head reminds me, for the thirtieth time today, that Caleb is the final bachelor. The one expected to bring in the largest donation.

"So what?" I grumble aloud, alone in my truck. *Great, now I'm talking to myself.*

It's not like Caleb Harlow hasn't had buckle bunnies throwing themselves at him for the last decade in his quick rise to bull riding-celebrity status. He just hasn't taken anyone up on their offer, or offers in many cases, since his accident. I should be happy for him, not annoyed. This event is to raise funds for a new vet for fuck's sake, so why wouldn't the best looking guy around help out?

Who wouldn't want to bid on a date with those big brown eyes? He'll bring in plenty of money for new equipment to attract a vet.

My phone vibrates in my pocket. Again.

Again, I ignore it.

Why is it that we've been practically inseparable since the accident and the thought of going to the auction makes me want to puke? What would I even do there? You don't bid on your best friend, not when there are throngs of fans lining up.

Especially not when you told him you're attracted to men as well as women over a month ago and nothing ever happened.

Thankfully, the parking lot comes into view and I refocus on helping my cousin. When I park, I finally look at my phone. It's only been ten minutes since I replied to Caleb's last message, right before I left the ranch, but I'm not surprised to see three new messages.

Caleb: Fiiiiiine. I'll be on my own tonight.

Caleb: But you could still come. I'd even add to the winning bid for an added date.

Oof. I feel like I was just sucker punched. Why would him adding me as a pity-date entice me to come?

Caleb: If you're really not coming, want to play video games at my place when it's done?

Three dots appear. He's typing again and I still don't have a reply.

Caleb: Did Courtney make me presentable?

A moment later, a picture comes through. It's perfect, of course. It looks like Tommy's best friend added a little product to define Caleb's natural dark curls, keeping them off his face.

It's smart, he can wear his hat and then wave it at the crowd without having hat hair. His eyes have gold flecks in them from the lighting, which means he must be outside. I've only noticed that gold shimmering when the sunlight is hitting his eyes.

I take a moment to drink in the rest of the selfie. He must have let Courtney shape his beard like I suggested. It's nice and close to his skin on his cheeks and a little fuller on his chin, his dark facial hair complementing his already tan skin, even though it's only May. The top few buttons of his shirt are open, a silver chain around his neck catching the light. Of course it only accentuates his sculpted pecs. Even after all that time recovering, he's already back in peak physical condition. My eyes are drawn to his mouth and the way his lips—

A knock on my window makes me drop my phone.

"Hey man, is it in the back?" Jesse's sweaty, but he doesn't look annoyed at my complete cluelessness of his approach. God, how long have I been gawking at a picture of the guy I see daily?

Nodding, I cut the engine and pick up my phone, locking it and putting it in my pocket without replying. My mouth waters when I open my door and the smells from Jesse's barbecue hit me.

"Damn, that smells amazing," I say, walking over to him and helping pull out the four-by-four that's halfway out of the truck bed already.

"It better. I've been roasting without the window open prepping the sides." Sweat drips down his temples. "It's like a damn sauna in there and my A/C went out in my truck the other day. I figured I had time before I'd really need it fixed."

"Sit in mine when we get this up while the food truck cools down. You should have almost an hour before people are here and I'll help get things set up."

God, anything to keep my mind off of this fucking auction.

Jesse's eyebrow raises and his gaze searches my face. "Are you a glutton for punishment all of a sudden?"

Rolling my eyes, I try to keep the agitation I can't shake over Caleb and this damn auction at bay. "If anyone with Landen blood has a chance at helping you out with food prep, you know it's me. Plus, you look like you're moments away from legitimately becoming a puddle."

"You're right about that," he says. "I suppose I shouldn't look a gift horse in the mouth."

We reach his food truck, the awning sitting flat over the window.

"Hold your end and I'll anchor mine against the tire." Jesse leans down and shifts a few larger rocks to keep the board snug and in place before pushing up the awning. "Okay, it should be able to sit in this corner without sliding out."

The board feels sturdy enough to keep the metal covering propped open most of the way and we step back to examine our work.

"Thanks, man," Jesse says, patting my back. "You're a real lifesaver. I think I would have passed out before everything was ready in that hot box."

I hold my hand out for him to lead the way into the food truck. "Think nothing of it, just show me what you'd like me to do and then go sit."

My brain immediately drifts to the picture of Caleb as Jesse points out a few things. What the hell is wrong with me? I'm here to help my cousin who is donating all of this food to sweeten the fundraiser and I'm all but moping because my best friend is helping raise money, too? Shit, now someone's calling me. I'd put money on Caleb.

"You going to get that?" Jesse asks, looking pointedly at my vibrating pocket. "I'm good unless you have any questions."

"Go rest and I'll take over." Jesse waits a moment and I hold back a groan of frustration while I pull out my phone and swipe to accept the call from Caleb.

Chapter 10
Caleb

"Are you okay?" I ask when the call connects as I step outside, getting away from the auction prep.

"Sorry, just helping Jesse with a few things," Matt says distractedly. There's a shuffling sound and I can hear his cousin's muffled voice get softer, like he just left. "Courtney did a great job."

I blink in confusion, trying to catch up.

"Um yeah. She did." Why did I need to call him to see if he was alright? Just because he didn't reply as quickly as usual? "What did Jesse need?"

"The awning for the food truck had a piece snap, so it could only lay flat against the window while he was prepping for tonight." He's moving things around, like he does when he's cooking at Landen Acres. I can imagine him in Jesse's small space, keeping everything going in a way that looks so natural. Besides being on a horse, I don't know that I've seen him be more comfortable anywhere than when he's in the kitchen. "I brought some boards to prop it open. I'm keeping his prep going while he cools off in my truck so he's on time for your date."

He sounds cranky. I suppose I would be too if I was the one standing in a hot box.

"Does that mean you're at the park?" I ask, keeping my hope tempered.

"Yeah."

"So, you're closer to town than you are to Landen Acres..." I let the silence stretch, waiting for him to take the hint. It's not like I've been subtle about wanting him at the auction.

After several long seconds, a non-committal grunt comes through the phone.

"Do you take pleasure in watching me squirm? Metaphorically speaking," I joke, my hand gripping the back of my neck.

"Why would I do that?" His tone is flat. Not the easy-going friend I've had for years.

"Did I do something, Matt?" I ask before I can think twice about it.

"What would you have done?" he counters, making my frustration mount.

"Why don't you tell me?" I ask.

Silence.

I'm used to giving Matt time to reply. Most people assume his silence is him being a dick, but he usually just needs ten seconds or so to pick his words. So I wait and count to twenty in my head just to be safe.

Nothing.

"Okay, so something happened?"

Matt scoffs. "No, nothing happened."

He's talking, that's good. The door opens next to me and Sarah, no, Samantha, taps her watch and holds up five fingers. I nod and give her a thumbs up. I'm well-aware this damn auction is starting soon and I'll be on a date shortly after. With someone I've likely met a few times already, but chances are I won't have a clue who they are.

"I don't know how to fix things if you don't talk to me." Desperation leaks into my voice and I bite my lip to stay quiet long enough for him to answer. My anxiety rises thinking of doing this stupid auction and not having Matt here.

It's fine that he doesn't want to bid on me for a date, even if it's a group date and not real. I can deal with that. It's just, God, he's been my rock through the accident and he's always just *here.* This is the first time I've *asked* him to be somewhere and he's made a dozen excuses. Now, he's clearly not at the ranch to help a supposedly new farrier, or needing to cook a batch of broth so nothing goes to waste from dinner last night, or even helping Chuck move some of the gym equipment because he wants space to jump rope. That last excuse died almost immediately since Chuck isn't even in town.

"You're being reckless." He's agitated when he says it and I can just imagine him shuffling food around in jerky motions. I wait a beat and assume he's not going to elaborate without some prodding.

"What do you mean?" I ask, keeping my tone even and calm so he doesn't shut down. A frustrated sound escapes him, and I can hear one long exhale before he replies.

"How tired are you?" he asks, surprising me.

"Not tired," I reply, confused. "Why?"

"Well, you're likely going to be after working at the ranch today and especially with the auction itself. Not to mention your headaches."

Ah, he's thinking I'll exacerbate my more acute symptoms tonight.

"You know the doc said I could do this," I remind him gently. "I'll be wearing my earplugs to dampen the noise and will keep my hat on while I'm on stage for the lights."

"Good, you're all set then." He pauses and lets out a sigh. "You'll be great, just..."

I wait, counting slowly to fifteen in my head this time.

"Just have fun and be careful. I'll see you tomorrow and you can tell me all about it." His voice is almost normal. Most people would think he was fine, but I can hear the slight strain he's trying to hide. God, I wish I could see him right now.

"You're not staying with Jesse for dinner and games?" I ask, heart sinking a little because I already know the answer.

"Nah, I'll head back home so he gets every bit of credit he deserves for this event."

"Yeah, okay," I say. "I'll, uh, see you tomorrow then."

Twice he takes a breath like he's going to say something.

But in the end, he only says goodbye and we hang up.

Chapter 11
Matt

With more force than necessary, I shove my phone back into my pocket and wipe the sweat threatening to drip into my eyes. Even with the window open and the fan running, it's hotter than sin in here. I don't know how Jesse does this in the summer. It's only May, so I can't imagine being in here under the scorching July sun.

Everything is looking, and smelling, good, so I can ease off my agitated shuffling and take a damn breath. It's hot and humid and only serves to piss me off. I need to find a way to not be in full dick-mode by the time Jesse cools off and returns.

What the fuck is my problem?

Stupid question. I know what my problem is. A few months ago, that first night in the hospital, Caleb hit on me, more accurately: came on to me, with a boldness and sexiness I haven't seen from him. It unlocked something in my heart that I've kept shut down for years. For a little while, I thought he might say something, anything, that hinted it was more than the painkillers talking.

But nothing.

I haven't held his hand again, too chickenshit for him to think I'm some buckle bunny trying to jump him. Not that I'm opposed to that.

Fuck. He's going on a date with someone tonight. He's getting back in the proverbial saddle. Just not with me. And I'm not someone who will be the pitied third wheel. I still don't know what he was thinking when he offered to add me to his date. How pathetic does he think I am?

Slightly cooler air enters my nose as I close my eyes and try to shift my thoughts. Looking out the open door, I see Jesse sitting in my truck with his head tipped back against the headrest. My hand snakes to my back pocket and pulls out my phone, unlocking it automatically. Because I'm a glutton for punishment, I pull up the picture Caleb sent and let my eyes take in the rest of the details. The little wrinkles next to his eyes are always a dead giveaway that his smile is genuine. His mustache follows the curves of his upper lip perfectly and his teeth are a pop of white against his complexion. I steal a glance at my truck and Jesse is still relaxed in the front. So, for once, I give voice to what's been beating in my heart for far too long.

"I wish you were mine."

I'm not sure how long I stand there, staring at his picture, but the sound of a door closing snaps me back to reality. God, I have to get my shit together so I'm not some love-sick fool pining after someone who threw me one single crumb while hopped up on painkillers. He's my best friend and I can focus on that. My heart can get over the idea of us being more. Of anyone being more, really. But not Caleb.

Jesse's boots snap a twig as I shoot off a quick *good luck* text to Caleb and close out of my messages, likely looking guilty. At least I didn't let anything burn, that I know for sure.

"I can't thank you enough, cousin," Jesse says, stepping into the small space and patting me on the back.

"It was nothing, really. I'm just glad you won't be passing out from heat exhaustion." I look around. "Anything else you'd like a hand with?"

"No, this was amazing. Seriously, this is the big event before my dad's back for a couple of weeks, so we'll get everything fixed properly before he's gone for his final work trip."

"What else needs fixing?" I ask.

"Not fixing, but we're putting in an actual air conditioning unit so this," he says, motioning to the general interior, "stays relatively manageable later this summer."

"Let us know if you two need a hand, okay?"

Jesse nods and we switch places so he can take over.

"And when Uncle Kent is back, you'll both come out to the ranch for dinner?" I ask.

"We might need a false pretense to get him there because telling him we're celebrating his early retirement might make him feel old."

My brows furrow. "I thought he was proud of being able to retire now."

"Oh he is," Jesse says. "He's still a little weird at parties since the divorce was final. He can meet with people from anywhere, but small town functions mean small talk with people he's known his whole life. I think he misses Mom running interference more than anything."

He's casual in his delivery, but he worries about both his parents. The divorce was pretty amicable, but his mom already moved in with someone about an hour away.

"We can say we're celebrating a horse Jax rehabbed or Gertrude's birthday."

"How is that cow?"

"Old," I snort.

"She's got to be at least fifteen," he says, shuffling a few things around in his fridge.

"At least," I agree. "I'm sure Chuck will host a blowout for her twentieth birthday. The entire town will be invited."

"And maybe the entire county," he adds.

A real smile tugs at my lips, and I feel lighter than I have all day.

"Thanks, man," I say, giving Jesse a nod.

"I'm the one who should be thanking you," he says.

"I know, but, ah..."

"You let me know if there's anything you'd like to talk about." He puts up a hand to stop my interjection. "I know you have four brothers and a best friend, but sometimes, you need someone else to talk to. Just throwing it out there *if* you need it."

Swallowing down the ten responses brushing off his offer, I just say, "Thanks, again."

"See you later, Matt."

Raising my hand in an awkward wave, I shuffle out of the food truck, breathing in air that feels less sticky, and hop down the steps. My mind takes over.

Maybe instead of talking to someone else about all these feelings, I should go to the auction? The next few steps I take help me rule out that plan of action. Nothing good would come from that. If things were reversed and I was on stage with Caleb winning the date with me, it would be the sign I was looking for. Unfortunately, as the youngest Landen brother, I wouldn't bring in a fraction of what he's bound to get tonight for the fundraiser.

The cold air shocks me a little when I open the driver's door to my truck and helps me switch gears. The best thing for me to do, is to continue to be there for Caleb as his best friend.

But when I try to find the courage to show up tonight and watch other people bid on a chance for a group date with him, my heart squeezes so painfully I have to catch my breath. Okay, so tonight isn't on the table, but I can see him tomorrow. Maybe surprise him with lunch so we can play video games at his place like he wanted to do tonight so he's not driving out to the ranch all the time.

The more I think about it, the better it sounds. I'll get up earlier than usual, get most of my work done before eleven, and then bring lunch to Caleb and hang out for a few hours playing videos like he was hoping to do tonight. I'll ask enough questions about the auction and the date to be polite without being suspicious, and everything will be perfect.

Chapter 12
Caleb

Crankiness isn't a good look for someone who just raised a ridiculous amount of money for the new veterinary equipment, but it's a struggle to keep it off my face. I remind myself that this is just like when I'm working a crowd after a ride or during the awards presentation. Well, now that we're at the park, I'm less on display and it feels like I'm trying to win over a potential sponsor. Except this lady already spent her money.

She's nice enough and is staying within the spirit of this group date. I've been in too many situations where it was clear someone thought they were getting something *more* from me. Thankfully, I always got out of leaving alone with someone I didn't want to be with, usually Cooper stepping in and closing out the tab for the evening and giving an excuse for me. He's definitely still sore from my decision to not list him as an emergency contact. He means well. Always has. But it's business. For emergencies, I want someone who cares and knows the real me. Not the guy everyone sees riding bulls.

"Isn't this the best chicken?" my date asks, pulling me back to the food in front of the full group and the fact I've only picked at what's on my plate.

"Oh yeah, it blows me away every time," I say, pulling out some of that charm I have deep inside. "Tell me more about yourself."

I really hope that she doesn't live in my apartment building or run the register at the grocery store I go to once or twice a week. She didn't say her name, so I keep avoiding using one, but I'm sure I've met her before. Maybe she came out to Landen Acres one day?

"Well, you already know that I work at the moving company." She smiles and I nod like it was something I definitely remembered. Damn, I couldn't even say it was a woman who organized things for the move let alone recognize her from that. "But I'm a runner and have my tenth marathon coming up in the fall. Do you run?"

So much for buying me time.

"I'm more of a bull rider and manual labor kind of guy." She gives me an inquisitive look. "I like to work with my hands so I'm out at Landen Acres a lot helping out with whatever they have going on."

"I'm sure they love having you there." She's not flirting with me, just genuine. I like that. I thought that's what Matt and I had. Well, maybe some flirting every now and then, especially on my part trying to tease out if I have a shot with him. But something genuine.

Today just feels like something is missing, or at least that I missed something.

My date gets up for another soda and I'm enough of a gentleman to wait for her back to face me to quickly look at my phone, just in case I didn't feel it vibrate. Just in case Matt messaged. The lock screen has no new notifications, but I open my messages just to confirm what I already know. Just a message wishing me luck.

Part of me itches to go over to Jax and Tommy to see if they know what's going on with Matt. They're at the far end of the table with Courtney and Jax's date. I think it's Chase's youngest sister, but I haven't seen her much before moving to Greenstone other than a few rodeos she tagged along for.

No, I don't need to bring my own insecurities to the fundraiser.

Maybe I've been clingy and around too much. Maybe Matt is sick of me. I suppose that could be it. He's taken care of me for too long and needs a breather. That's something I can give him. It doesn't matter if he doesn't want more, I'll take whatever he's comfortable with. Maybe it's time I be more independent with my life in Greenstone.

Once everything is in the pot, I give it one last stir and start the shower. The jog felt good. If I see my "date" again, I'll have to tell her that our conversation got me off my ass and instead of my regular routine to keep my muscles toned, I went outside for some fresh air completely on my own, just for myself.

Stripping down as the shower starts steaming, I take a moment to look at my reflection. My scars are so much smaller now, especially the one on my shoulder. I rotate my arm and wince on reflex when tendons tug in resistance. The pain has been gone, but my body still has its own memories in addition to those I've replayed of that night.

Before stepping into the shower, I look at my phone. Still nothing from Matt. I stop myself from sending him something. No, today is about giving him the space he clearly needs.

The water feels incredible running over my sweat-slicked skin, the warmth relaxing my muscles. My brain has a mind of its own in this space and today is no different. When I close my eyes, last night replays, but instead of the runner, it's Matt walking up to me after Sam closes the auction. Matt who sits beside me on the bus.

Except, unlike my date last night, his pinky casually brushes against mine during the dinner and my breath catches. I don't dare move as I watch, transfixed, as it slips over mine with a quiet authority. One that only comes out every now and then, but one I've imagined in far too many situations. My eyes find his as I let him tug my hand and entwine our fingers.

My phone rings and buzzes aggressively against the counter. A low groan of frustration leaves my throat and I'm back in the shower, one hand on the wall, the other fisting my dick, aching for release.

"Get it together, man," I say, changing the settings so the water is cold, but not freezing, relieving me of the haze of desire. With more vigorous motions than necessary, I get clean and grab my towel the second the water is off. My skin pebbles from the chill and the effects from the cold shower are almost negated when I see the missed call.

Matt.

Two new messages, as well. When I reach for the phone to see what he said, it rings again. This time, I answer immediately.

"Hey," I say.

"You okay?" he asks right away.

"Yeah, just got out of the shower."

"I'm here, want to let me in?"

He's here? Now?

"Yeah," I say again and shake my head gently. "One minute."

"Alright, bye."

I hang up without saying anything else, my mind going right back to that bus ride that never happened. I look down at the water dripping down my chest and smirk.

If Matt's not interested, that's just fine and I'll respect it. But I'm definitely aware of the effect I have on people and maybe in my rush to let him inside, I'll only have time to partially dry myself, toss some mousse in my hair, and oops... I might forget my shirt.

Chapter 13
Matt

"Be his supportive best friend, not a jealous, lovesick puppy," I remind myself as my boots click in the entryway of the building. The nerves I keep pushing down bubble right back up with each step I take.

"For fuck's sake, get a grip," I whisper, making a mental note to stop talking aloud to myself, especially in semi-public places. Unfortunately, Caleb's apartment isn't far down the hall so I'm knocking on his door much sooner than I hoped. The lock turns and in a panic, I stare down at my boots and feel the canvas tote bump against my leg. What if he wasn't in the shower by himself and his date is still here?

My mind doesn't have more time to spiral because the door opens and I see one pair of bare feet with gray sweatpants brushing the tops. His toenails are kind of long, so I focus on his toes for a second before letting my eyes travel upwards, bracing myself for a second set of feet to come into view.

Thankfully, all I can see are these damn sweatpants. The material shifts a little and he leans against the doorframe, pulling my focus towards his hips, but I get caught on the outline of his dick. My throat goes dry and I try to swallow as I stare, like a fucking fool, where the ridge presses against the fabric.

There's a chance I let out a tiny whimper.

This is mortifying, I know what's happening, but my eyes just slowly make their way upwards to where the waistband sits low on his hips and his skin glistens where they create a defined V. More toned skin is exposed the higher I look and there's a trail of water dripping over his nipple and down the side of his abs.

Jesus, it's not like I haven't seen this man shirtless before. In fact, it was just three days ago at the ranch. I don't know what's wrong with me, but I can't look away. I feel like a drowning man taking his last breath of air before he goes under, waiting for him to confirm my fears that the group date set him up with the love of his life. Which I know is irrational. Even standing here in the hallway like a buffoon, I know that.

Caleb clears his throat as I'm taking in the details of the stallion tattooed on his pec and my eyes snap to his, a smug look on his face.

I can only imagine the shades of red my face is turning, but instead of making things more awkward, I say the first thing that comes to mind.

"I'm here to play video games and eat," I grumble. "You need to trim your toenails."

Then I step across his threshold, bracing myself for evidence of another person. No extra shoes by the door. No clothes strewn about. No dishes out. The couch looks normal, the blanket folded neatly over the back and the cushions where Caleb sits are the only ones with indents.

"I guess they could use one," Caleb laughs, shutting the door. He walks by me as I take off my boots, his scent washing over me for a moment before he gives a view of his backside and the way his muscles flex as he moves.

Suddenly, alarm bells go off in my head, bringing me back to earth and not this slow-motion porno I'm living in.

"What's burning?" I ask, dropping the bag and rushing into his familiar home.

Caleb curses and lunges towards the kitchen with me hot on his heels. He flounders in front of his stove where there's a pot with smoke pushing out from under the lid.

This, I can handle. I step between Caleb and the mysterious meal, turning off the burner so the flames don't do more damage. He always has two towels hanging from his oven door, a light one for drying your hands, and a dark one for drying dishes, and I grab the closest one to shield my hand from the heat of the pot and move it to the back burner. Before turning back to Caleb, I reach up and turn on his vent fan to clear some of the smoke. It's not too bad, mostly smelly and not enough to set off an alarm.

I'm about to give him the same smug look he gave me a moment ago, but what I see wipes it off my face on the spot.

Caleb leans against his counter with his head tipped back and his hands covering his face. Frustration radiates off him in waves and I close the small distance. My hand reaches up and gently tugs his fingers, and I ignore the spark deep in my belly at the contact that's so intimate to me. I stop my mind from bringing me back to the night of his accident and how it felt to fall asleep with his hand in mine. How that's the only time anyone's hand in mine has ever felt right.

"Talk to me," I say calmly, knowing he needs to feel safe and not judged for however this happened. My fingers beg to linger, but I don't want to crowd him. I take a small step back and he drops his other hand from his face.

"I was an idiot." His jaw clenches shut when he finishes the sentence.

"What happened?" I prod.

Caleb deflates with a sigh but looks at me. "I forgot to turn down the damn burner before getting into the shower and then I got more distracted when you called saying you were coming over and I wasn't dressed."

"You're not exactly dressed now," I say, trying to bring him out of this funk I've seen so many times. He rolls his eyes at my comment.

"You're the one who noticed," he says with a half smirk.

"In my defense, right before you got to the door, I realized you might have someone here with you."

"Who else would be here besides you?" he asks, his face scrunching in confusion. Then it shifts to amused, making me think I must be showing my relief somehow.

"Um, maybe we can meal plan and do food prep together so you're not cooking alone as things continue to improve," I suggest. "They *are* getting better, Cay, and they'll continue to."

He nods and grips the counter, making his forearms bulge with tension. "Yeah, we can do that."

Instead of feeling pity, which is what Caleb likely thinks, my heart pounds in my chest just thinking about having more time one-on-one with Caleb. In close quarters.

I can't tell if I just signed myself up for pure torture, or heaven on earth.

Chapter 14
Caleb

I'm not sure when I was ever this embarrassed. Here I am, shirtless and damp all thanks to my plan to lure Matt into confessing his undying devotion to me, standing in my kitchen where I burned soup.

Soup.

He hasn't lifted the lid, thank all that is holy. But while I preened at the way he slowly took in the sight of me only wearing the first pair of sweatpants I could grab, I burned soup.

All because I didn't remember to turn the burner down before leaving the kitchen to shower.

All because of my fucking TBI. The scars, physical therapy, and counseling all did wonders for me after the accident, but the injury to my brain still has lingering symptoms, namely memory shit.

"Hey," Matt says, the concern in his eyes making me want to crawl in a hole. "We've got this."

We.

He's here with me and whatever happened yesterday, he's figured out. It's not worth pushing him for something more and messing up what we have. Even if he did ogle me in a way I'll definitely be thinking about in the shower tomorrow.

"Yeah, we do," I reply. "What's in your bag?"

"It's a surprise lunch." That fucking smile. The one that kicks up to the right, hiding a few of his freckles on that cheek. God, that smile could talk me into doing so many things.

Trying to keep any ruefulness out of my laugh at how this whole situation went from Matt checking me out to him rescuing my apartment from burning soup, I say, "You always seem to know what I'm going to need."

I sober quickly, thinking of how I needed him last night. No, I *wanted* him last night. Wanted him to show me...*something*.

"Let's see what we're feasting on," I say, gesturing towards the door where he dropped the bag when this all went south.

"Grab some drinks, plates, and three forks and I'll meet you on the couch." He throws me a wink.

Oh fuck me. I have to cool down and go into my room for a moment. He's going to kill me with his attempts to distract me from the no-longer-smoking soup.

Fucking flirting disaster. I do my best to *not* slam my drawer shut after grabbing the shirt on top while trying to release some of this frustration without being obvious to Matt. I give myself a second, resting my hands on top of the tall dresser, letting my neck relax and my head hang low between my biceps. My breath leaves my nose in increasingly calmer exhales and by the fourth, I feel more put together.

"Beer or cider?" I ask him, leaving the safety of my room.

"Hard cider, please," he calls back while rustling through whatever he's brought.

Grabbing two bottles of his favorite kind of cider, which sits next to his favorite kind of beer, from the fridge, I get some glasses and everything else he asked for.

When I come around to the living room, he already has things set out. It smells fantastic, a mixture of soy, ginger, garlic, and cilantro.

"Wow." I don't really have other words.

"Chicken potstickers and Pad Thai with a twist," he explains excitedly. "And then lime, crushed peanuts, bean sprouts, and cilantro to add."

"Damn, this looks amazing. When did you make all this?"

A hand reaches behind his neck and pink colors his cheeks. "Um, I got up a little early for prep."

There's no way that's the whole story. Even when he gets up early, he doesn't have time to cook something like this until later in the afternoon.

"Uh-huh."

"Shut up," he mumbles.

"Just how early did you wake up?" I prod, possibly wanting to gain a little dignity back.

"I made you lunch," he states.

"That doesn't answer my question," I counter.

"Nope, it doesn't," he says enthusiastically, making me chuckle. "Now give me one of the forks and I'll dish us up."

"Alright," I say, handing him a fork then opening the caps of the ciders. I pour them into the two glasses while Matt fills our plates and opens a few small containers I didn't notice.

"You made these, too?" I ask, nodding at the three different sauces.

"Yes." His tone is a mix of exasperation and embarrassment.

Damn, he went all out for this. Even though part of me wants to keep needling him about how much time he put into this impromptu lunch, I switch gears. "Which one should I start with?"

"This one." He points to the sauce with the lightest color. "It's a little sweeter, but has more ginger than the other two, so I think you'll like that combination the most. But the darker one is a sesame-soy and the lighter sauce has a stronger garlic kick. I think you'll actually like something about all of them."

My throat gets a little tight hearing that. He made three different dipping sauces for lunch. Three sauces that go with the meal thinking that I would like all of them. No one has ever known me as well as Matthew Landen.

"You just made me want to try all three at once," I say, trying to keep things light.

"Oh gross. Don't mix them."

At his seriousness, I burst out laughing. "I didn't mean mixing them, I meant that you made them all sound amazing. Pass me the sweet ginger one and I'll start there."

Instead of handing me the sauce, he drizzles some over one end of a potsticker on my plate then looks at me expectantly. I stab the food with my fork and take a bite. My eyes close and I let out a moan. The flavors explode on my tongue with the sweetness of the sauce balancing the savoriness of the potsticker. It's phenomenal. The slow-burn heat from the ginger hits my tastebuds a moment later.

"So," Matt says. "Does that mean you like it?"

"I fucking love it," I say, taking a second bite while looking into his blue eyes. He holds my gaze and something shifts—just a little in his expression before he gives me a half-grin.

"Thank God." The words are said like he was talking only to himself so I lean towards him and put my hand on his forearm.

"Really, you shouldn't be worried about my opinion on your cooking. But for what it's worth, you've blown me away with my first two bites and I'm ready to scarf down the rest."

"Savor, you should be ready to *savor* the rest. Not scarf."

Well, I can think of one thing that I'd like to savor for the rest of my damn life.

Chapter 15
Matt

Listening to Caleb moan with pleasure as he tastes the final sauce I made is doing too many things to my body. One specific area to be exact, which is making sitting in jeans incredibly uncomfortable.

It's always been hard to take my eyes off him, but it's practically impossible now. Especially whenever his tongue darts out to catch some sauce that's dripping.

"Aren't you going to eat?" Caleb's voice pulls me out of my pathetic staring. Thankfully, he only seems to have noticed that I haven't taken a bite of my food versus my inability to look away.

"Definitely, I just wanted to make sure you have everything you need."

"What more could I need?" He gestures to his plate so I know it's not a question loaded with double meaning, but something in his eyes almost looks like yearning if I didn't know any better. It gives me the smallest bit of courage to prod so I can stop wondering.

"Maybe your date from last night?"

He laughs. "Sure, if I remembered her name."

He's definitely deflecting, but names are especially hard for him to remember now.

"So, what *do* you remember about her?" I ask, wanting to be supportive in case he does want to see her again.

"She's a runner, and talking to her got me off my ass this morning and out for a run myself." A little twinge of unwarranted jealousy pinches my gut as he continues. "She's about to do another marathon and she works for the moving company we used."

"Oh, you mean Cora Kennedy?"

Caleb mumbles something I can't quite make out. Likely something about my memory functioning.

"Honestly? I have no idea. But if Cora Kennedy is the scheduler for the moving company and she runs marathons, then she's likely the woman I had Jesse's barbecue chicken with last night." He takes his first bite of his noodle and curses. "I'm not putting down your cousin's cooking, because it's fantastic, but I don't know what the hell you put in this to make it taste so damn good. How are you not eating it?"

Shit. What is wrong with me? I shove one of the potstickers into my mouth, skipping the sauces in my haste.

A lopsided grin waits for me when I look up. "I thought we were *savoring* and not scarfing, Matthew."

He's messing with me. But hearing him say *Matthew* like that has desire flooding my system again and something inside of me becomes still. My focus is on Caleb and nothing else exists. The air between us seems to crackle and if he gave me *some* sign that he wanted me even a fraction of how much I want him...

The things I would do with him.

My hands ache to run through his hair. My heart pounds with its need to have him near. My lips long for just one taste.

No, not just one. I know if I were to ever taste Caleb Harlow, stopping would be sheer agony.

"Now you're not eating," I say, my voice rough.

His lips part, drawing my attention there. God I want to claim them with mine and have them wrapped around my—

My phone vibrates, jarring me out of this moment as Tommy's name flashes on my screen. I look back at Caleb who is now frowning at my phone.

"He doesn't usually call during the day." Caleb's voice is a little worried, reflecting my thoughts. I answer the phone and put it on speaker.

"Hey, what's up?"

There's a shuffling sound and Tommy's voice is far away as he says, "One second, Chuck tied a string to the bottom of the chair and the wheel just got stuck in it."

"Is everyone okay?" I ask, feeling less worried and more confused.

"Yeah, why wouldn't they be?" He's closer to the phone again, which is always helpful.

"You never call me, especially not during the day."

"Oh, sorry, no emergency. I was calling to see if you could pick a few things up since you're in town?"

"Of course, what do you need?" I ask. Caleb swats my leg and holds his unlocked phone out to me so I can text the list to myself. There's a little star next to my name since I'm an emergency contact and it makes my stomach do a flip knowing no one else's name has one.

Tommy rattles off a mix of groceries for restocking the cabins farther out on the property and a few things to grab from the supply store. Caleb nudges me and mouths *Why didn't he text you this?*

I shrug, feeling just as lost.

"Is that everything?" I ask.

"Yep," he says. "Are you still at Caleb's?"

"I've been eavesdropping this whole time," Caleb chimes in, scooting closer so our knees are almost touching.

"Hey man, I was hoping I'd catch you. Sorry that I didn't really get to talk to you last night. How was your time with Cora?"

"She was nice." Caleb coughs a little and grabs his glass and takes a swig, his Adam's apple bobbing with each swallow.

"Y'all okay over there?" Tommy asks.

"Must've gotten something down the wrong tube, that's all." He clears his throat. "But she really was nice. We talked a lot and she's going to do her tenth marathon so it got me off my lazy ass this morning to go for a run myself."

"That's great. Are you going to see her again?"

Why was it so easy for my brother to ask the question I wanted the answer to this whole time?

Caleb's eyes flick towards me so fast I almost second guess that it happened. "Uh, I don't think so? I'll see her around town, I suppose, but we didn't make plans to go out or anything, if that's what you're asking."

"I was just curious if the rodeo star was ready to settle down for good," Tommy says.

"I'm ready to stay here in Greenstone, if that answers at least part of your question." He rubs the back of his neck and looks down at his plate. Tommy continues to chat with Caleb about other things from last night's barbecue. I remind myself to relax and act normal. Things have already been awkward enough with what happened when Caleb answered the door dripping and shirtless.

Chapter 16
Caleb

There's nothing like having your crush's brother ask you if you're going to go on a date with someone else. On speakerphone, nonetheless.

"Can we set a place for you tonight?" Tommy asks.

I have to stop myself from looking to Matt to see if he'd like me there. He brought lunch for us and it's not like I'm not friends with all five Landen brothers...

"Yeah, I'll help Matt with the errands and then follow him to the ranch." Taking another swig of my cider, I sneak a glance at Matt, who looks a little...relieved?

I get it. I'd rather have my best friend than the distance that saturated the last twenty-four hours. It's time to make sure I'm contributing to life here in Greenstone and on the ranch so he's not being drained by how much I've needed him.

My libido will calm down. Until that happens, I'll remind myself how shitty life feels with Matt avoiding me. At some point, someone else should catch my eye, right?

Tommy talks to both of us a little longer and adds a couple of things to the list. When Matt hangs up, we start eating again but something feels different. Not tense, but not normal.

Breaking the silence, I pause with my fork halfway to my mouth and ask, "Are we okay?"

Matt blinks a few times and gives me a soft smile, drawing my attention to his lips. Lips that I've dreamed of claiming with mine. Lips that I've imagined wrapped around—

"We're okay."

God, my mind can't keep going there. Forcing myself to nod like I wasn't just thinking of Matt on his knees, I say, "Good."

Things feel a little easier. Not quite back to normal, but I'll take it.

When we've polished off almost everything, Matt gets up to fill the dishwasher. I stop him with a raised eyebrow. "You brought a feast. The least I can do is clean up at my own house."

"Says the guy who cleans up at our house all the time." Matt holds his plate high in the air so I can't reach it without jumping.

"You just love showing off that you're a few inches taller than me, don't you? Come on, let's clean up."

Matt gestures for me to lead the way and he follows just behind me. I open my small dishwasher, put my dishes in, and reach back for Matt's. When my hand remains empty I shift so I'm looking up at him. His expression is expectant, like he's waiting for me to figure things out.

"What? Give me your plate." My fingers wiggle and Matt chuckles.

"Fine," he says, passing his plate over, but keeping his fork.

My hand goes back out for that. This time, he waits until I look at him again. He easily flips the fork between his dexterous fingers, the same thing Tommy does with his pens when he needs to fidget. Then he lowers the fork down so the end of the handle traces one of the lines on my palm.

I couldn't even move if I wanted to right now. Matt's eyes have me frozen in place as he presses the fork into my hand, achingly slow, allowing skin contact I wasn't expecting. His fingers leaving a trail of fire in their wake.

Then he gives me a smirk, turns around, and I release the breath I was holding.

What the fuck? If he had shown up last night, I would have thought he was flirting with me, but…he didn't. *Wouldn't.*

I absolutely shouldn't, but as he walks away, I watch his ass, noticing, not for the first time, how well his jeans always hug it perfectly. Scrubbing my hands over my face, I reset myself before closing the dishwasher and standing up.

"I'm taking this out," Matt says matter-of-factly, lifting the bag in my recycling bin and tying it shut as I mutter a thanks. I know the tone he has that brokers no argument when he wants to handle something.

He opens the top cupboard to get a new bag for the bin, tucking the edges in exactly how I do it. My heart gives a painful squeeze as I think of how easy certain things could be. With all the time we've spent together since my injury, we've learned the little details of how we each function and it shows.

"Give me a minute to throw on jeans and we'll head out. We'll play video games next time," I say, turning to my bedroom as Matt gathers his containers into his tote. He gives me a nod and I shut the door.

I step out of my sweats, fold them, and put them back in their drawer. Opting for my well-worn jeans, I pull those on and grab my favorite belt. I've earned plenty of buckles from rodeos over the years, but this buckle is the first I won. Every time I fasten it around my waist, I'm reminded of everything that prize got me. I was already independent, but was scraping by and earning my keep with odd jobs, but I was free of my family. This win was the first time I felt ahead of the game for my finances.

I'm tempted to check the current state of my investments. I know I have more in savings and investments than I'll ever need, but I keep waiting for it to be taken away. Waiting for my family to figure out where I went and what I do stopped being a worry years ago. No one in that small town cared about the rodeo, so moving over a thousand miles away, changing my number, and never having my own social media seems to have done the trick. It didn't hurt having Cooper gatekeeping all my contact information while I got more and more media coverage, either.

Maybe one day I'll be able to use it to build a life with someone.

Running my hand through my wavy hair, trying to tame it a little now that it's dry, I leave my bedroom. Matt's sitting on the couch, checking something on his phone. He looks comfortable with one arm propped on the back of the couch and his ankle resting on his knee.

"Ready to go?" he asks quietly without looking up.

"I didn't think you knew I was out here."

He puts his phone away and stands up, grabbing his bag. "I always know."

Then he winks.

Again.

Fuck.

Chapter 17
Matt

He's wearing that belt buckle. The one that always draws my eyes, making it look like I'm checking out his crotch. My self-restraint might be slipping more than I'd like as we spend time together every day, but at least I don't usually do *that*.

It's not like I don't know the story behind the buckle and why it's well-worn. It's like his truck, it reminds him of how far he's come, completely on his own. I look in the rear view mirror for the umpteenth time, seeing that his left arm is still hanging out of his open window. I don't know why he likes that on the highway. My windows are rolled up and my arms aren't being pummeled by the wind.

Turning down the main gravel road, I drive under the archway with the Landen Acres logo. It's looking a little worn, reminding me of the last time it was updated. Fifteen-year-old me was quite the ass, but somehow, Dad's patience was endless that morning as I griped about everything from the ladders, the drills, the bolts, the sun, my jeans, or my gloves. But we got it done and he was so proud that I had done it with him.

It's not long before we're pulling into the garage to the west of the house, Caleb parking outside even though we've all told him to use the garage. He comes around the corner, getting a wagon to haul the specialty feed a few of the horses need. We work in tandem, first emptying the bags from the bed of my truck and then his.

Caleb has on a T-shirt that his biceps fill perfectly when he throws each bag on our pile. When he climbs into the bed of his truck to get the second row of bags there, his jeans stretch tight over his ass and I make sure I'm busy inspecting something on the cart before he turns around.

"Everything good?" he asks, one bag already propped up against his knee. "We can split this into two loads if we need."

"No, we're all set. Pass it down."

Caleb kicks his knee up and grunts as he swings it to the edge of the tailgate. He tips it into my arms before getting the next ready while I add this one to our pile. I try to focus on the burn in my arms as we make quick work of this, but each grunt he makes has my mind imagining the sounds he'd make with someone sucking him off. No, not just anyone. Me.

Especially since he told Tommy he wasn't going to go out with Cora. I realize that he could be interested in someone else, but that was the first date he's been on in probably a year. There are people throwing themselves at him on the rodeo circuit and I'm not naive enough to think he turns all of them down, but there wasn't anyone who seemed to be a repeat. Whenever we go out, he might dance a little, but he politely declines any other offers. And some of them are very generous.

He jumps down and closes the tailgate with a loud *clang*. I push the back of the wagon to rock it to gain some momentum and Caleb plants his feet to help. Our rhythm matches automatically and it's only a few moments before the wheels move forward. We take advantage of our forward movement and I jog to the front and grab the handle to pull with him. Our pinkies press together as I begin to sweat. Usually, when we're deep into ranch chores, we make contact like this, but we have our work gloves on. Right now, I don't have to imagine how his skin feels against mine, even though it's such a tiny point of contact.

Caleb's eyes dart down to our hands, but he doesn't make any adjustments. The handle isn't very big, so if he wanted to have more space, he'd need to switch his grip.

"Are you okay staying for dinner?"

"As long as I don't have to cook, I'm in," Caleb says, glancing at me with a nervous smile.

"Whatever you'd like to do, or not do." I don't mention that I'm not the one cooking dinner because if he'd like to try not burning something, any of my brothers would be happy to let him join.

"It's up to me?" He raises an eyebrow, looking sexy as hell.

"Sure," I say, shrugging.

"You've been scheduling most of my activities lately so I haven't had to."

"And usually you're pretty happy with that," I counter.

"I can't deny that." A chuckle escapes his lips and I swear it shouldn't affect me half as much as it does, because...damn. "But I'm in."

A low string of curses comes from around the corner and we enter the stables only to see Bryant scrubbing at his shirt.

"I think you're making it worse," I point out.

"I'm well aware," he says, throwing the rag into the garbage. "I wasn't paying attention, didn't cap the conditioner and knocked it over when I started working on the saddle."

"That's not like you." Caleb frowns.

"It was a boneheaded, rookie mistake," Bryant says, peeling off his shirt and using the cleaner side of it to wipe off his stomach.

"Is everything okay?" I ask. Bryant isn't exactly someone who shares his feelings, but he seems more ornery than usual.

Unsurprisingly, I get a grunt in return instead of a real answer.

"You'll tell us what you need, right?" Caleb tries to make eye contact with my burly brother.

"Sure," he snorts.

When Caleb looks back at me, I roll my eyes and nod towards the storage area for the feed. We tug on the wagon to get it rocking only to have Bryant walk up to us with his arms crossed over his chest.

"Yes?" I ask.

He waves us away with a flick of his hand. Caleb chuckles as Bryant takes the handle from us and without even a peep, he gets the wagon rolling.

"Should we follow?" Caleb whispers. Bryant can be hard to read, even for me at times.

"Nah, he's in a mood. I wouldn't be surprised if he gives half the guys the rest of the day off just so he has an excuse to work off whatever's bothering him."

"Did he run out of wood to split?" He walks up to the Appaloosa here for training and rubs her forehead. I rode her the other day in one of the larger corrals while he rode Jax's horse Misty, who might be the calmest horse I've ever known. It hits me how much he looks at home here on the ranch.

But I can't think like that.

Like he might make a home here...with me.

So instead of joining him, I walk past to the next stall to check that the mare has plenty of water and joke, "I think we still have a few hundred acres with trees for him to work through."

One day, his answering laugh won't be something I feel from my head to my toes.

Chapter 18
Caleb

The only thing that could make things feel *just right*, is Matt having his arms around me. Or Matt doing just about anything with me, for that matter.

Instead, he's checking on a chestnut mare in the next stall while I rub the Appaloosa's nose.

Well, maybe riding one of these horses would be even better.

Taking a step back, I pull out my phone and shoot a note to my doctors asking if I can do more than gentle riding soon because I'm itching to really get into the saddle again.

It's not like I need to get on a bull or bronco, but letting the horse canter would feel normal.

I could use more normal.

Once my phone is safely back in my pocket, I look up to see Matt's back to me. He's reaching in and touching the back of the horse, causing him to lean forward.

Damn, his ass looks amazing.

I close my eyes and remind myself that we're just friends. Really good friends. And I want things to stay that way.

Unless he tells me he has feelings for me.

My eyes snap open and my heart pounds when I hear a horse nicker.

"That's it, girl, I've got you," he practically coos.

Approaching calmly so I don't spook the mare as he does something I can't see, I speak encouraging words to her. When I'm close enough, I hold out my hand and she nudges it with her nose, and I take it as a sign that I can pet her.

God, it always feels amazing to be with horses. Even more so since the accident. They've been an escape for me since I turned ten and was first introduced to riding through a neighbor. I think I was able to stay with my family as long as I did because I had that outlet.

Well, I stayed as long as I could to make sure my sisters were okay, but they took after our parents and never understood what a healthy relationship with family should look like. That familiar ache starts up. It's not quite *loss* over what I had that's now gone, but more a feeling of regret for what never was.

A family who cared for one another. Especially one who didn't just see you as a means for bringing in cash they could spend.

Thinking about the past won't change a damn thing though. Because of everything that happened, I'm here, on this ranch, in front of this beautiful mare, standing next to a man who feels like home. And that scares the shit out of me because I haven't wanted anything like I want *him*.

The corded muscles of his forearm shift as I watch while he's doing something on her back until he pulls away and straightens up.

"There you go, girl," he says. His hand rubbing the spot just below where my hand is just as I'm dropping mine down towards the mare's nose.

There's a pause where neither of us move. Nothing more than a fleeting moment, but long enough that it seems that the only thing I can see or feel is his hand touching mine. It's something that sends a wave of sensation through my whole body even though it's such a small bit of contact.

While my body is buzzing with the rightness I feel right now, he clears his throat and gently scratches between the horse's eyes. I give her nose one last rub and take a small step back, taking in the sights, sounds, and smells surrounding me.

Being around horses has always been the place I've felt the most like myself when I needed to get away. Away from the constant arguments over when I was going to start bringing in my "fair share" to cover the family's bills before I was a teenager. The non-stop disappointment when I had the audacity to stay in high school as long as I did rather than work sixty-plus hours each week like they expected. All while my parents bounced from one job to another. All while pushing their oldest out of the house at five in the morning, telling him he better be working seven or eight hours each day on top of being a sixth grader. I can still hear them telling me I wasn't welcome in the house until I had done that every damn day.

"What are you thinking about?" Matt's voice pulls me from an unwelcome trip down memory lane.

"My first jobs," I reply.

"Oh yeah? I don't think I know what they were." He leaves it as a statement. He knows I'm not always open to talking about my life before joining the rodeo, but he knows the basics.

"Odd jobs here and there where I'd run errands for older people before school, and then after school I washed a lot of dishes."

"All off the books?" he asks, likely sensing something in my tone.

"You know it," I say, letting out a long breath. "It's not a good look to have someone who was legally still a child on the payroll. But most people knew my dad and must've taken pity on me."

"I'm sorry." His hand reaches towards mine for a moment before he lets it drop. I know he's not a touchy-feely kind of person so just the fact he reached is meaningful.

"The most fucked up part is that I kept feeling like I was supposed to be sending money back to them for the first full year after I got out of there."

"I take it they wouldn't have just thanked you and left you alone?" he asks.

"Bingo. There was nothing but greed in them."

"Yeah, but they raised you," he says with a shrug.

It's such a simple statement implying there's enough good in me that it had to come from somewhere.

"They raised me to be selfish and fight for what I wanted. I'm grateful for that because if they hadn't, I would have never left."

"But you did. You got out of there and now look at what you've done with your life, man. You're in a place where you can retire before you're thirty."

"That's a very kind way of putting it. I've been thinking that it was more of an unplanned medical leave that turned permanent." I chuckle and keep things light. "I'm twenty-eight, single, and almost burned my apartment down today."

"That's all you see now?"

I don't know how to respond. At the time, it felt like self-deprecating humor, but maybe I've really been seeing myself that way more than I realize.

There's chatter in another part of the stables and I'm reminded we're practically out in the open and here I am talking about my family. If there's one thing I've been careful to keep out of the spotlight, it's them.

Matt glances towards the voices before he speaks again. "Have you ever been in the loft?"

His question surprises me but brings relief.

"I haven't." I don't think I've really seen anyone go up there.

"Let's change that now." He gives a little nod towards an almost-perfectly-vertical ladder nearby.

"What's up there?" I ask.

"Hay," he says, grinning back at me as he grips the old ladder. So much of the stables have been updated and replaced, but the ladder seems to have seen better days.

If there was anything I was going to respond with, it leaves my head immediately as he climbs the ladder right in front of me. His shirt tightens each time he reaches up and his jeans hug his ass like they were painted on.

"This ladder is twice as old as Jax, but I promise it can handle plenty more than the two of us," he says as he pauses and looks over his flexed shoulder at me. "Come on."

I rub my hands together like I'm preparing myself mentally to play into the fact he thinks I was hesitant to follow.

It's probably a good idea not to have your best friend catch you checking him out regularly.

Chapter 19
Matt

I'm not *bringing him up here to seduce him.*
I'm not *bringing him up here to seduce him.*
But God, I want to.

I repeat that to myself as I ascend the final few rungs of the ladder and step onto the straw-laden floor. This isn't a place I ever brought anyone I was seeing, but I know some of my brothers did, especially as teens. I always understood the appeal though as it's quieter, away from the business of the main house, and used to be partially full of bales of hay for storage until a big remodel, leaving a smaller space. We finished up that work just before Dad passed.

As Caleb's hat comes into view, I reach my hand down and we grab each other's wrists so I can help him maneuver from the ladder to the loft. Just like everything, it feels right. I don't even want to pull away. We're not holding hands or anything, but it's close enough to where I'd usually be wanting to yank mine free as soon as possible. But that's not the case here. In fact, I'd rather slip my fingers through his again, and that has my heart pounding in my chest.

Then I picture him on the stage at the auction and imagine all the people enthusiastically bidding on spending a few hours with him. On a group date no less.

That's enough to bring me right back to reality.

Because he's a famous, gorgeous, charming, rodeo king.

And I'm just Matt.

"It's bigger than I expected," he comments, looking around the space.

A laugh escapes me before I can stop it. My mind is in the gutter with what I've imagined doing with him in this very loft and it would have been nice to not make that evident.

He's got a cocky grin as he says, "I can't tell if you're laughing because it's a phrase you've heard before, or one you haven't."

Oh shit, has he thought about—

"Wouldn't you like to know?" Somehow, I manage to sound nonchalant as I avoid eye contact because he's not flirting with me, he's giving me shit. Just like best friends do. So, I sit down on one of the few bales up here and pat the bale once for him to join me.

"Why is there so much loose straw?"

My foot shuffles some straw so we can see the floorboards. "This loft was created before bales were standard so it's not built to hold a bunch of bales. You've likely been in stables that are newer than this one so the lofts could handle heavier storage."

He rubs his chin, his fingers making a scratching sound against his beard. "I don't think I've been in a loft before."

"Really?"

"Really. I don't remember the one stable near the house growing up having a loft, so when I'd work to pay for riding the horses, I never went up to get anything."

"Well, you can come up here whenever you'd like."

"How old is the flooring?" he asks, examining the now-gray board showing.

"Old," I say, chuckling. "But the boards have been replaced over the years, we just haven't added the support for storing more up here since we have plenty of space without having to climb a ladder."

He shifts so his back is against the wall, his hat resting on the bale on the far side of him. "It's nice up here."

I stop myself from saying something about it being musty because he seems so relaxed.

"It's quieter, but I can still hear the horses."

"You miss the rodeo?" I ask.

One eyebrow raises as he looks at me. "It's all I've known for ten years."

"That's not a real answer."

"I don't think I'm used to being away from it, yet." He looks at the exposed rafters, probably noticing the dirt and grime that has built up over the years. I've visited where he trained and it was a top notch facility with state of the art equipment. It was so different from this place that, while it has a long and proud history, has been updated in waves as funds allowed.

"I never dreamed I'd be able to pick where I'd settle down, but I hoped it would be a place like this."

I do my best to not latch onto what he says because he doesn't mean *this* ranch.

But still, his words surprise me a little.

"I assumed you'd shift to training the next generation of riders and build a house with lots of open space and big windows."

"You remember what kind of house I want?" he asks, a lazy grin on his handsome face.

"It wasn't hard," I say, leaning forward to rest my elbows on my thighs.

"Why is that?"

Shrugging, I say, "Because it matches what I want."

It must be my imagination going into overdrive, but I think I hear him take in a sharp breath and go still. His hand falls between us on the bale and, again, I want to hold it.

God damn it.

This is my best friend still healing from a traumatic injury sitting next to me.

As much as I'd like him to be up here on a date with me, he's not. On top of that, he's entrusted me with helping make medical decisions and I'm not about to let my feelings break that trust.

No matter how strong those feelings are and how much they're growing every damn day we spend with each other.

I need to get my head on right or I'm going to fuck up our friendship by being bitter over him not wanting me. Hell, I'm the youngest of five brothers who somehow can't keep anyone around other than said brothers.

He looks at ease sitting here right now. "You know you can come here any time you want, right?"

"Who else comes up here?"

"Now that we're all out of school, mostly just me."

"Ah," he says knowingly. "Who brought the most dates up here?"

"Chuck," I reply without having to think twice, earning me a laugh.

"I could see that."

"Jax barely brought anyone around even when he was in high school and that hasn't changed. We all caught Tommy up here with his ex a few times, and Bryant once with someone from out of town. Chuck, on the other hand, seemed to find a certain charm in bringing people back to fool around in the loft."

"And you didn't?" His tone is a little more careful than I'd expect. Normally, he'd be joking with me about my brothers, but something is weighing on him that I can't read.

"God no," I say. "I've never done anything at the ranch besides making out behind closed doors."

A frown appears on his face. "I thought you had, um, experience—"

"*At the ranch* was the key phrase," I say, chuckling. "I've seen my brothers catch each other enough times that I avoided them like the plague when I was younger."

"And now?"

Shrugging, I give myself the freedom to tell him the truth. "Now the person who I wouldn't care about getting caught with isn't exactly interested."

"Well, it's their loss," he says, leaning forward and putting his hat back on.

"Yeah, their loss."

If he only knew...

Chapter 20
Caleb

One Week Later

After catching my reflection in the mirror near the door, I go back to the bathroom, wet my hands, and run my fingers through my hair.

For some reason, I thought brushing my hair after it dried would be a great idea. It seemed okay when I was doing it, but my hair really turned into a fluffball. With static.

Realizing that damp fingers aren't going to undo the damage, I cup my hands under the running water and dip my hair down into the little well I've made. Once everything is wet, I towel dry my hair as usual and put away the brush.

Fuck, I'm way more nervous than I should be right now. It's not like Matt coming over is something new.

But he had me pick up a comically long list of groceries for a bunch of meal-prepping.

So I'm less likely to start a fire in my apartment.

Matt: Parked and leaving my truck.

I buzz him in and unlock the door, leaving it propped open. In the short time it takes him to come in, I haven't found something else to do.

Great, now it looks like I've been waiting for him.

At least I've been able to keep my usual staring to a minimum the past few days. Or so I thought.

Because he is one tall drink of water.

God damn it, being around him was supposed to get easier. But every fucking time he's near, I just want to crush my lips against his and finally taste him.

"Is everything okay?" he asks.

Get a grip.

"Yeah, sorry, just spaced out for a second." I reach for the tote he's carrying and our fingers brush while I take it from him.

It's torture, plain and simple.

The barest hint of a touch has me weak in the knees.

"Do you need to rest?" Concern makes his brow knit while he slips out of his boots.

"Nah, just had my mind on the wrong thing," I say, turning away from him and walking to the kitchen. "Let's get cooking."

"Okay, you'll tell me if you need to take a break, right?"

"You know I've been making good progress and my stamina is way better now."

He turns beet red. Was it because I talked about my stamina? I'm going to drive myself crazy trying to find any sign that he wants me half as much as I want him.

"But yes, I promise I'll tell you if I need to take a nap, chef."

He makes a choked sound before loudly clearing his throat as the blush spreads to the tips of his ears.

Interesting. I might have found a nickname for Matt.

It's not long before we have way too many ingredients out along with my saucepan, stock pot, skillet, and baking sheets. Did I know the difference between a saucepan and a skillet? Not a few minutes ago. But Matt says it's important to use them for their intended purposes so I'll try to remember.

"Let's start by chopping up the onions and celery," he says, tossing an onion my way. "We'll use these for a few of the dishes."

"Alright," I say, peeling off the top layers and whacking it in half.

Matt is completely still and staring at me.

"What?"

He blows out a breath and looks at the ceiling.

"How did you learn to cook?" he asks, barely holding back a wince.

"Me?"

He mutters something under his breath. "Okay, let's rewind a second and talk about how to hold your knife."

He keeps talking me through what to do, but the moment he reaches over my cutting board and puts his hand over mine, my brain short circuits and all I can do is feel his touch. The way his calluses press down on the back of my hand has my mouth going dry. The feel of his fingers taking control around mine has my heart thumping.

Then he starts to move the knife with strong, sure movements and I know I'm completely gone.

"One sec," he says, taking his hand off mine, breaking the spell, and I take a gulp of air trying to recenter myself into a coherent human being.

But then I feel the heat from his body just behind me and his hand is back, only this time, his whole arm presses down on mine.

I vaguely hear the words, "Grip the onion," while his other hand forms mine into a claw. I can only imagine that this is so

I'm holding the onion safely but I'm trying to remember how to breathe right now and that seems like a feat in itself.

He efficiently slices the onion a few different ways before chopping it.

Fuck, his hands make quick work of the onion and suddenly he releases me.

"Now you try that with the other half."

All I can do is blink at him for a few seconds. I don't dare turn my whole body to face him because he'll see just how much he affects me.

"Sorry, I just went through a lot of instructions at once and should have broken it down better," he quickly says. "Why don't you start by grabbing the other half of the onion and setting it upright to make the cuts that don't go all the way through."

Some part of my brain must have paid attention to more than the overwhelming sensations that bombarded me while being surrounded by him because I'm able to do that.

"Good. Watch the grip on your knife, you're holding it like your life depends on it."

I loosen how I'm holding it but can't remember any of his instructions. "Like this?"

"Almost." He reaches across and adjusts my hand so the knife sits more naturally against my palm. "There."

Focus.

The knife makes shallow cuts in the onion the long way.

"You can go a little deeper, actually, then you'll have less to chop at the end."

Holding back a groan at hearing him talk to me about going deeper, I do just as he says.

My pants tighten, nonetheless.

When I'm done prepping the onion, I start chopping it and his hand covers mine almost immediately.

"Hang on, it's easier if you press the tip down on the cutting board and use a rocking motion."

I'm so screwed.

Chapter 21
Matt

Thankfully, Caleb only seems a little overwhelmed by all my instructions and isn't calling me out for being borderline inappropriate with my word choices. It's not like I'm trying to say things with double meanings, but I can't seem to stop them from coming out of my mouth.

This might have been a terrible idea to do at his place. Alone.

At least at the ranch, Tommy would likely be in the office and anyone could walk in.

But no, I arranged to do all of this here at Caleb's apartment because it's all for him.

"Like this?" he asks, his voice a little rough.

My God, I'm going to have to leave the kitchen soon to cool down and we've literally just started.

"Yeah," I say. "Just like that."

And then my brain catches up with what I said.

Great, I'm right back in the world where everything I say sounds like I'm either having sex, or about to.

Needing to get my mind off the way it felt to have my arms closing him in and my hands enveloping his, I put three onions next to his cutting board. "Want to do these as well?"

"Sure," he says, focusing on using the curve of the knife's edge to rock the blade just like I showed him and finding a smooth rhythm.

"Alright, I'll rinse the celery off and will get going on that." Honestly, I can't tell if I'm explaining what I'm doing for his benefit or my own at this point. I've never cooked this closely with someone else.

Or rather, I've never cooked with someone I was borderline desperate to be with before.

I continue babbling about what I'm doing, reminding myself that there's a specific purpose to what we're doing and this isn't one excuse after another for me to make contact with Caleb. It would be easy enough to get lost in the fantasy that we're together and this is our life. Just the two of us doing everyday things together, without any barriers between us.

No reason to not touch each other.

No reason to not lean over and claim his lips with mine.

But that's not real life.

At least it's not mine.

My life is with my brothers and not romancing the pants off a rodeo star who made pretty quick work of the remaining onions.

We continue chopping vegetables and putting them in bowls as we go. When it's time to start cooking, I only start one burner, so he can focus on the first dish alone.

Maybe I was too ambitious with everything I planned for today and instead of prepping for the week, we should have just worked on one or two things and used prepared foods to supplement.

He uses the back of his hand to push his curls off his forehead while grabbing butter from the fridge and an ache forms in my chest. I know he'd never settle for a guy like me.

But in little moments like this, it's so easy to picture how it *could* be. What it might be like if I wasn't the youngest brother who drove our mother away. If I wasn't a burden when our father passed because I needed a guardian. If I wasn't...me.

If I had the confidence of Chuck.

If I had the smarts of Tommy.

If I had the good looks of Jax.

If I had the presence of Bryant.

Maybe then, I'd stand a chance at catching Caleb's eye as someone worth a second look. But as it stands, I'm none of those things and he's probably ready to settle down with someone.

Just not me.

Jesus, I need to get over this one-person pity party that I'm throwing myself over here.

"Matthew?"

"Shit," I say, setting the skillet back onto the heat after tossing the onions into the air a few times. "I kind of went into autopilot there for a minute, sorry."

"Don't apologize, I can see what you're doing just fine." He shifts so his hip is resting against the counter, arms folded across his chest, and his necklace catching the light. "Will you show me how you do that without having onions flying all over the kitchen?"

Is he asking me to show him how to hold the handle of the skillet and jerk it back quickly?

This has to be a test, right? Something to see how long I can go before I break.

"Sure," I say before talking him through the actions, trying to avoid words that make it sound like I'm constantly thinking about getting him naked.

Pretty soon, he's trying it and I'm watching him grip the handle of the skillet with his big hand, doing a motion I want to see again and again.

I have got to get it together.

"Keep them moving every so often and watch them so they don't burn, and I'll be back in a minute," I say, hightailing it to the bathroom and sending a glare at the pillow Chuck got him only to see that Caleb really did tape a note so it reads *save a horse,* gently *ride a cowboy.*

My glare instantly goes away as I snort out a laugh, loving his humor.

I stop in my tracks in the doorway to the bathroom.

Nope, not loving.

Fuck.

I cannot be in love with a guy who can have anyone. A guy who sees me as a friend.

Shutting the door firmly, I turn on the faucet so the cold water is running at full blast and start splashing my face again and again as my heart constricts.

I can't lose him, too.

Then a small voice buried deep in my heart asks, *But what if you don't?*

With the water still running, I grip the sides of the sink, steadying myself.

"What if I don't lose him? Yeah right. Even if he shared my feelings, why the hell would he want to stay with me?"

And now I'm mumbling to myself about a hypothetical relationship with the man I left in the kitchen.

I take a deep breath, trying to calm myself out of a downward spiral.

Reminding myself of some of my therapy session mantras, I whisper a few out loud as I look in the mirror, my face still dripping wet.

"I am enough as I am."

Deep breath.

"I am worthy of love."

Deep breath.

My chest loosens to where I feel semi-normal.

Damn, this little trip took a messed-up turn quickly.

But I don't have to do anything right now other than get back out to the kitchen and meal prep with Caleb so he's not burning the shit out of his meals.

No declarations of feelings.

Just being myself.

He needs his friend and I know, at least on that front, I'm enough for him.

"You've got this," I say to my reflection while drying my face. "Just go back in there and be—"

A quiet knock on the door shuts me right up.

Oh fuck, what did he hear?

Chapter 22
Caleb

There's quiet cursing on the other side.

"Sorry, I just heard your voice and wanted to make sure you're alright," I say.

"I'm okay. I'll be out in a minute." His voice is muffled, like his hands are over his mouth or something.

"Alright. I'll, uh, go back to the kitchen then. Take your time."

Take your time?

What is wrong with me?

He was probably on his phone, actually.

I frown because he never leaves to talk to someone. Why would he feel the need to hide from me?

Shit, maybe he's seeing someone.

I'll have to pretend to be happy for him because it's my own damn fault for not telling him how I feel. God, I've had so long to say something, but there was always an excuse.

He's only twenty-two.

He'd have to be away from the ranch to see you.

You'll have photos online with other people and gossip that would drive even the most confident partner away.

He's your best friend.

With more force than necessary, I toss the onions like he showed me and turn the heat back on. At least I remembered to turn off the burner when I left the kitchen.

My phone vibrates and I pull it out of my pocket to see a new message from my agent.

Cooper: Hey Caleb, we have a few endorsements to reply to in the next week, were you able to look at them?

I sigh because no, I haven't looked at them. Not really.

"Are you okay?" Matt asks from just outside the kitchen. I didn't hear him come back.

"It's Cooper, I have to get back to him about some jobs."

"You don't sound happy about it," he says, coming in a few steps and leaning against the cabinets with his arms crossed. The neck of his shirt is a little damp. The same is true about the hair that falls over his forehead, but I don't say anything. "What's the job?"

"A few endorsements, so commercials and ads." I shrug like that's a normal thing everyday people in small towns deal with.

"What's the hold-up?" He looks at me with a scrutinizing gaze.

"They're usually in the capital, but one is in New York and when I glanced at the details, they're all spread out so I'd be gone for a bit."

"Is there a reason to take them?"

"It would make Cooper happy."

"Well, if you're going to stay in the rodeo world, maybe you should keep Cooper happy."

"What if I'm ready for something different?" I ask, looking down at my phone just to have something to do other than stare into his blue eyes.

"Like settling down?" His voice is scratchy and deep.

"Yeah."

"Are you fully ready to leave the rodeo?"

"Maybe," I say, knowing it's a huge decision.

Who am I without the rodeo?

He crosses in front of me and tends to the onions.

Because I forgot about them.

Fuck, what good am I going to be to anyone if I can't even cook for myself without messing things up? How can I compete with someone who grew up on a damn ranch and doesn't need their hand held so they don't burn down their apartment building?

"We can go over the details later today or we can have Tommy look them over, too, to see what you might need."

"My finances are fine," I say absentmindedly. The guys have full access to my regular bank account but that's just a drop in the bucket.

"Your hospital bills haven't been small."

"I have plenty of investments." He looks at me with an eyebrow raised. "I wasn't kidding any time I talked about retiring."

"Well, then it comes down to what you want. It sounds like you don't want to travel, so if any of these sound intriguing, can things be done around here for the promos? It could be worth asking."

"What do you think I should do?"

Tell me to leave it all behind and stay.

"I mean, you know how I felt about you doing the auction, so it might be too soon to jump into all of that with the travel and shooting depending on the schedules. But if you like the brands and if your long-term goal is to possibly ride again, then I'd say you should see if they're flexible."

"So you think I should ask for time and do it?" I ask.

He opens his mouth and closes it, taking his time to figure out what he wants to say. The onions catch his attention once more.

"Since these are getting soft, we can add the celery. Next time, we'll cook them on a higher heat so this won't take as long." He smoothly moves around the kitchen, scraping the chopped celery off the cutting board and into the pan and efficiently mixing them in with the onions with a few tugs of the pan.

Then he clears his throat, stuffing both hands into his front pockets. "What do you want?"

I wait for the rest of the question for a moment and realize that's it. I can't tell if he's asking only about these gigs, the rodeo, or life in general. Fortunately, there's only one response that I want to say more than anything.

You.

But I can't find the courage to say it right now. Not if it means messing this up. Not if there's the slightest chance he's seeing someone and keeping it a secret.

"I want to put down roots. I want to ride again, but I don't want my life to only be about that." I take a small step towards him. "I want to belong somewhere and not have to constantly earn my place."

Close the distance, please.

"You've more than earned all of that, Cay," he says softly, staying at the oven.

"I'm tired. And no, I don't need a nap," I add with a smile. "I'm just...tired."

"Then reply to Cooper and tell him you're passing. I'm sure there will be more opportunities that you can accept, negotiate something you'd rather have, or just pass on." I type as he continues. "And in the meantime, Bryant was asking me the other day if you might be interested in riding at the ranch. When you're ready, of course."

"What do you mean?"

"We usually have horses that are getting ready to be saddled or need work getting back into one after an incident. Bryant was thinking you'd be the perfect person to have around—not only for that, but we could expand and offer lessons and things like that. You know, if Greenstone is where you'd like to stay."

"What does everyone else think?" I ask, hoping he'll see right through the question and tell me what *he* thinks.

"What's not to agree with? We'd all lo—uh, like to have you around more."

Hope spreads through me.

They're offering me a place to belong.

Something I'm good at where I could contribute to what they do.

"I'd like that," I say. "I'll be sure to talk to the doc about what I need to do before I can really ride."

Matt tries to hide a smile while he tosses the celery and onions again before he says, "Good."

I can figure things out.

Worst case scenario, Matt is my best friend and I get to work alongside him and his brothers.

Best case scenario, we ride off into the sunset together and build a life somewhere on Landen Acres.

I can live with either.

Chapter 23
Matt

One month later

Damn, he looks good on a horse. Everything is so natural. The moment he sticks one foot in the stirrup it's like he was born to be in the saddle.

Every time we've gone riding, he's grumbled about the helmet, but that's a non-negotiable for the foreseeable future, much to his dismay.

"Pretend you're on a bull, Cay," I call out as he fiddles with the strap once more.

"Yeah, yeah," he says with a dramatic eye roll. "You'd be tugging at it for a regular ride, too, and you know it."

"I can jump off and grab myself one if it'll make you feel better." The offer is sincere. There's no one around right now so I don't think he's feeling too self-conscious about having the helmet on, but if it would ease his mind and help him relax, I'd do it without a second thought.

"No, that will just make me more aware of it if I see you in one. Which way?"

"Take the trail to the left at the fork and I'll lead when we need to veer off it."

"Are you sure you don't want to lead right away?" he asks, looking back at me.

"I'm sure, now let's get going."

He flashes me a grin right before he urges Bella into a canter on the narrow, well-worn path. I wanted him to go first so he felt more freedom on this ride. Since he's still getting used to the trails around the ranch, he's been following one of us so he doesn't get lost or turned around.

But he's been told what to do so much in the past few months that he needs to not feel like he's being held back. That he can handle things himself.

Today, he asked me to bring him to the place I mentioned once, probably a year ago, where I'd like to build a small place for myself. I haven't talked to my brothers about it though.

It's not that I think they wouldn't approve of me having something that's mine. I just don't ever want them to think that I'm not grateful for everything they've done for me. That living in the main house isn't enough.

Telling Caleb was easy. He was excited for me and still is. But it's been Bryant, Chuck, Tommy, and me in the main house for years. Before our dad passed, everything was run by him and after, we kind of became a collective where no one makes big decisions without talking to the other three brothers. It's a good system, actually.

I'd just like to have something that's mine.

After a bit, I call out to Caleb because it's time to leave the trail. He slows Bella so it's easy for me to ride beside him for a moment.

"How do you know when to turn off the path?" he asks, looking at the trees around us.

"There's a boulder on the left side of the trail that we just passed. You continue on to the bend just ahead then you'll see a spot to the right where things open up for an easy ride."

"Didn't you say you've driven there?"

For a guy who's been struggling with memory issues since his accident, there are little details he seems to hold on tight to.

"There's an ATV path that I've veered off of a few times to get there, but the shortest route for that is to start at Jax's place."

"One second." He slows Bella almost to a stop, pulls out his phone, and I wait.

It's not like him to be on it on rides, or while we're talking. Maybe I shouldn't be annoyed, but I am.

Even so, I wait for him to finish whatever was so important it couldn't wait until we got to the place he asked me to show him.

"Sorry," he says, slipping the phone back into his front pocket and giving me a smile that shouldn't cause my heart rate to ratchet up because I still want to be annoyed. But damn, it does something to me every time. Especially when his eyes light up like that. He looks around and sees we're at the opening. "Well, what are we waiting for? Let's go."

He sounds like an excited kid who is about to get a surprise they've been waiting weeks for. I hold back a snarky remark about how we were only waiting for him to finish up with his sudden business and instead issue a challenge.

"Think you can keep up?"

That smile turns downright sexy as he replies with a simple, "Hell yeah."

And with that, I click my tongue and tap my feet against my stallion's sides, steering him off the main path and letting him work his way into a gallop. Caleb lets out a *whoop* and a moment later he's coaxed Bella right alongside us. She's shorter than Bandit, but she's one of the smoothest rides you can find.

I wish I was riding my Scarlett, but I promised Bryant I would get Bandit out for a long ride today since he's going home next week. He's calm and steady, like Scarlett, but needed to have his confidence built back up after an accident. I'd say he's going to do just fine with how comfortable he is with Bella so close. He's not second-guessing anything as I urge him to go through a shallow creek and doesn't slow until I ask him to.

By the time we've stopped the horses, their breathing is heavy, but not too labored, and they have a bright look in their eyes that only comes after the freedom of a run like that. I imagine mine have the same look because I see it in Caleb's, too.

He hands his reins over once I dismount and reaches for the strap on his helmet while he's still on Bella.

"Stop that," I chide, trying to keep my voice light. "You know you have to get down first."

"Yes, chef," he says, making it difficult for me to ignore how that phrase coming from his mouth affects the fit of my jeans.

Thankfully, I can use tying up the horses as an excuse to face away from him when he dismounts and adjust myself, making things significantly less obvious.

When I turn around, he's standing there, in the middle of the small clearing on top of a little rise on the property, helmet discarded at his feet, and a hand running through his brown curls. His back is to me, but I can see just how at-peace he is without seeing his face.

Maybe it was a mistake to bring him here.

Because watching him in the place I've dreamt of being my own little haven makes me hope for something I won't ever have.

Him.

Chapter 24
Caleb

"It's perfect."

Those are two words I didn't think I'd say and mean about any place.

But it is.

Perfect.

"I know." Matt stays half a step behind me, like he wants me to be able to take everything in.

I pull out my phone and snap a few pictures and pretend to go through them while quietly dropping a pin in my map app just like I did before we turned off the trail. This is Matt's favorite place and I don't ever want to forget how to get here.

Being at the top of this small slope gives an incredible view of just how big Landen Acres really is. I know I can't see everything from here, the trees are dense enough to the south and west to block the main house and stables, along with Jax's place and his smaller buildings. But there's enough of a clearing going down the hill that allows you to see the mountains in the distance, more forested patches, the large pond where I've gone swimming once this summer already, and even the grazing grounds for Chuck's cattle.

"I still haven't met the herd," I say, pointing to where I can see their small forms moving about.

Matt checks the time before saying, "We can go today if we leave fairly soon."

As much as I'd like to spend a couple hours here alone with Matt, another extended ride sounds amazing. Even with the damn helmet.

"I'd like that."

The more time I spend here, especially with him, the easier it is to feel the pull to stay. To belong. It makes me wonder, again, about the phone call he took that day in my apartment. He hasn't said anything about meeting up with someone and we've been practically inseparable. Maybe it wasn't the mystery person who he said isn't interested in him.

Maybe he's ready to move on.

I know that I can't put all my hope into finally being with him. But I can't help...hoping.

Hoping that this place could one day be *our* home. A place that is perfect, where I get to wake up every morning with my best friend as my partner, my lover.

I sit down in the long grass that I can imagine us arguing over whose turn it is to mow. A dog, for sure. One that we rescue as a puppy. It wouldn't roam as far as Gerald, but it would run along with us as we rode to the main house each day for chores. We'd still eat meals with his brothers, but we'd come home to this.

Some of the grass bends towards me as he lowers himself to the ground. His cologne mixes with the scents all around us, like this is meant to be where we end up.

Maybe it's this place and all that I see in it, but I find the courage to ask him something. Not everything I want to know, but something.

"Are you seeing anyone?" I'm so nervous that I have to look down at the calluses forming again. My palms smoothed out so much I barely recognized them by the time I moved to Greenstone. It feels good to have them back.

He barks out a laugh. "Sorry, I wasn't expecting that."

I shrug, trying to play it off that his response doesn't have me hanging on his every word. "Just being here and seeing what you want makes me curious."

"And when would I be seeing someone that you wouldn't know about?"

Of course he's going to make this harder than it has to be and not answer the question definitively. "I don't know, you could be sexting with someone in another state."

"Do you really take me for the sexting type?"

It's my turn to laugh. "No."

"I like a more hands-on approach than sending dick pics."

A choked sound escapes me and I play it off as a laugh because Jesus Christ, all I'm going to think of tonight is what that means.

"So that's a no?" I ask after a beat.

"That's a no," he replies with a cocky grin. "Are you?"

"Nope."

But God I wish I was.

"So neither of us have been sneaking around in the middle of the night," he says with a chuckle. "That's good to know."

I nudge him with my shoulder since he's so close. "Things are different now that we don't need to catch up or send each other regular updates."

"True," he muses. "It's different not having you on the road most of the year. But I'm not complaining about having you around."

We sit in amicable silence for a bit longer, a gentle breeze blowing through the trees and making the tall grass around us sway.

"Well, I get it."

He turns to look at me, confused. "What do you mean?"

"This," I say, sweeping one hand in front of me. "I get why this is where you want to settle."

He hums a sound of agreement. "One day I'll talk to my brothers about it."

"What's the hold up?"

A sigh escapes him while he decides what to say and I wait patiently.

"I don't want to seem ungrateful." He picks at a piece of grass as he continues. "I'm not sure if that makes sense, but I worry if I tell my brothers that I want to live tucked away on the property, away from them, that they might either think I'm sick of living with them, or that I'm, well, somehow ungrateful for everything they've done for me."

I know that telling him his worries are unfounded wouldn't help at all, so I try to imagine how it felt not only for Matt, but the other four Landen brothers, particularly after their dad passed. What was it like for them all to be worrying if Matt was going to be able to stay on the ranch or if he'd need to leave Greenstone altogether?

They'd sent me updates, but they were all dealing with their own grief and shock and so I didn't get too many details.

"What happened when Jax first brought up moving out?"

"Our dad was around so there was only one person who needed to sign off on the build. Plus, I was still in high school then."

"Didn't you all talk about it?"

He bends his knee and rests an elbow on it. "Yeah, but I don't remember a lot of the details. I just remember being half surprised and half unsure what that meant. Deep down I knew someone would eventually move out and with Jax craving quiet and solitude, it made sense that he was the one."

"Was anyone upset with him?" I ask, trying to lead him to remember what I hope was an event where everyone was supportive. But I wasn't there. I do remember getting updates on the house being built and then Chuck messaged me when Bryant brought their dad's cat out to Jax's place because it missed him. Actually, it was a video of it meowing incessantly at the door and a grouchy, shirtless, and, at that time, sporting his first ink, Bryant stomping out from his room. Chuck sent me a montage of Bryant gathering up all the cat's gear without a word, taking it to his truck, and driving away.

"Not that I can recall," Matt replies, reminding me that I asked him a question.

"Then you shouldn't expect less whenever you're ready to tell them what you'd like." It sounds simple when I say it, but I know it's anything but simple in his head. I'm just hoping to make sure he's not holding back on getting what he wants on the off chance his brothers, who would do anything for him, aren't going to like the request.

"I'll remember that," he says. "You sound a lot like my therapist. You know that?"

"She must be a genius," I say, winking and standing up. "Well, if we're going to introduce me to Chuck's ladies, we should get back in the saddle."

Before he needs to remind me, I pick up the helmet and secure it. Just like all the others with Matt on the ranch, the ride out here felt incredible. My body thrums with excitement looking out over the expanse we'll be going through to get to the herd.

"Alright, let's hope Gertrude is easy to find. Chuck would hate it if you went to meet his ladies and didn't get to see his true love."

"Perfect, lead the way, I'll be right there with you," I say, meaning so much more than this ride.

Chapter 25
Matt

If something doesn't happen to change how Caleb looks to me soon, I'm going to crack under the pressure of not coming onto him.

I know how terrible an idea it would be for me to do anything more than attempting to flirt every now and then or trying to get him to tell me something that could give me hope or finally shut things down. Yes, he's older than me, but I'm the one he trusts with his life. He continues to fill me in and ask my opinion on what the doctors say after his visits. I still go to appointments from time to time.

I need him to know that I'm here for him no matter what. That I haven't been showing up just to try to get into his pants. Hopefully, he'll never be hospitalized for something similar ever again, but whether we're just friends or more, I'll be there with him every step of the way.

Thankfully, he's putting his helmet on before mounting the horse this time.

"How many cattle do you have this year?" he asks, approaching Bella with an outreached hand which she nudges with her nose.

Untying the horses, I look over my shoulder towards where the herd is grazing. "It's somewhere around fifty. So it's still pretty small."

"And Chuck would like more, right?"

"You paid attention at dinner the other night."

"Of course I did. I like this place more and more as I get to spend time here."

You could truly be part of it. Even more than helping with the horses.

"You've been fitting in just like we all thought you would."

He lifts one leg to slip his foot into the stirrup, pulling his jeans skin-tight over his ass. I know I'm staring. But it's like I'm watching him jump up in slow motion. Everything is smooth and confident, evidence of spending years riding horses.

I pass the reins up to him, our fingers brushing lightly. Neither of us pulls back quickly, but we don't linger. Whatever sign I'm hoping for won't be coming so I need to act naturally, like he doesn't affect me with his touch.

Bandit huffs out a breath, pulling me away from Caleb, and my head clears of the heady feeling I get around the cowboy.

Once I'm in the saddle, I take one more look around, memorizing the sight of Caleb Harlow on a horse on this little piece of land that I'd like to claim as my own. It would be easier to make any sort of headway into getting over him if he didn't fit so seamlessly into life on the ranch.

"Are you ready to meet Chuck's ladies?"

"Yes, chef," he replies with a slight upturn of his mouth.

At least this ride will give me time to focus on something other than that phrase leaving his lips, which seem to be begging to be thoroughly kissed.

"Okay, let's go."

We urge our horses forward, Bandit trying to stay half a body length in front of Bella this time. Caleb's cheeks pinken from the wind whipping at his face the closer we get to the fence line, and I catch him grinning throughout the ride.

We dismount and he has his helmet off before he takes a single step away from Bella, keeping the reins in one hand. He wraps the leather around one fence post as I do the same at another.

Obviously, he's great with horses, but everything he does around them is automatic and smooth, it's hard to keep your eyes on anything else. No wonder his popularity quickly skyrocketed in the rodeo. Not only was he winning just about everything he could compete in, but it was like the entire stadium couldn't take their eyes off him when he was around.

Hell, I missed seeing full rides when he'd stand at the gate to watch someone else.

"Do I see a flower behind that cow's ear?" he asks, turning towards me and pointing just to the right of where we are.

Sure enough, there's Gertrude looking over at us, likely curious who Caleb is.

"You most certainly do," I say, clapping him on the shoulder and walking to the gate, hearing his footsteps behind me. "Chuck spoils her rotten and brings her a new flower every day. If he's out of town for something, he has one of us do it and has us send him a picture."

"You're serious."

"Completely," I reply, getting us through the gate and latching it closed. "No one exaggerates when we say this is Chuck's herd and that Gertrude is his."

"She's pretty, that's for sure."

Her long reddish hair covers her eyes as usual, but she pushes her nose towards me as I get close. "I'm sure she'll let you pet her, just let her smell you first."

My fingers tangle in her hair as I pet my way from her nose to the top of her back and give her a nice scratch while she takes a step Caleb's way, curious as ever.

"She's the only cow like this that you have, right?" he asks as she sniffs his fingertips and then his palm, pressing down into it.

"That's her signal that you're okay to pet her," I tell him. "And yes, she's the only Highland. Chuck would love to tell you the story about her over dinner some time, I'm sure."

My brother could brag about the mud caked to her right hoof, he loves this cow so much, and telling people how they found each other is something he loves to share.

"I'll have to ask him then." He smiles and starts speaking softly just to Gertrude, using her name regularly and staying in her line of sight.

Of course he instantly connects with every animal here, just another sign that he could really be happy settling and staying for good.

"Can I ask you something?" His voice is still pretty quiet so at first I thought he was talking to Gertrude, but he looks nervous now.

"Of course."

"Well, I need some advice, actually." He takes a deep breath and lets it out while focusing on Gertrude. "Like I said earlier, I'm not seeing anyone."

Another pause.

"But there's a person I'd like to, no, that's not the right wording." He lets out a frustrated *humph* before trying again. "I'm interested in someone but my relationship with them is complicated, but not really at the same time. Oh God, I don't know how to explain this."

So there is someone he wants.

Great.

Now I get to put my supportive-best-friend hat on and stuff my disappointment deep down inside while he's carefully touching the flower in Gertrude's hair.

"You like someone," I say, trying to get him back on track and hoping we can speed this suddenly painful conversation along.

"Yeah, I do, but I'm afraid if I say something, I'll fuck things up. I want to somehow let them know, on the off-chance they might be interested—"

Only a fool wouldn't be interested.

"—without making them feel like they have to do anything. Something where if they'd like to try being together, they can let me know, but if they don't, they can just not say anything and I'll know and can try to move on and stay friends."

"Have you given them any indication you want to be together?" I ask, watching him stare at the flower my brother put on Gertrude and getting a sour feeling in my stomach.

He lets out a rueful laugh. "Nothing that has worked, apparently, because I'm completely at a loss on how they might feel."

"Do you see them regularly?" My heart squeezes in anticipation of his answer.

"Daily," he replies, confirming the suspicion building.

It's Chuck. It has to be. He hadn't brought this up until seeing what a softie the guy is and he can't stop staring at that flower behind Gertrude's ear.

I never stood a chance because he wants to be with my brother. The one the same age as him. The one with all the charisma. The fun one.

"You could leave this person a note with some flowers. Just outside their door." Then Chuck can use the flowers over the next week for Gertrude.

Waste not, want not.

"What should the note say?" This time, he looks up at me with a mixture of hope and fear in his eyes.

Be his best friend.

"Something about how you," I pause to clear my throat, "feel and that if they don't return your feelings, to pretend this never happened."

There, I just gave him good advice while my heart is actively breaking. Just because Chuck seems interested in the new vet, doesn't mean he'd say no to Caleb.

He nods and pulls out his phone. "I like that, it's simple, meaningful, but gives him an out without having to say anything."

Him.

Seeing him with my brother might just push me to move out of the house sooner than I thought.

Chapter 26
Caleb

One week later

Shit, I've definitely bitten off more than I can chew with this mare. She's bucking more than she has been lately while saddled, which doesn't bode well for me getting on. Plus, she's not even out of the stables, yet.

My entire body is tingling with the anticipation of riding something that's trying to throw me off while a small part of my brain is yelling at me for being stupid. That the doctor was not thinking of *this* when they said riding was okay with a helmet.

Did they say I needed to stay off of a horse like this?

Not technically.

They said I should use my judgment and proceed with caution.

This mare has accepted wearing a saddle and now it's time for someone to ride her and my fingers are twitching to grab those reins.

The mud my boots keep sinking into can't dampen my spirits. Even if the distance Matt has kept between us tries to.

I've been trying to figure out what's been eating at him, but he seems to be a little withdrawn from everyone.

Maybe it wasn't a good idea to leave that bundle of wildflowers, that I tied with a twine that reminded me of the ropes not only from the rodeo, but what he uses here at the ranch, along with a note outside his room just before we went out. But after our conversation the day I met the famous Gertrude, I've been thinking nonstop about how to word the letter. I agonized every night over how to keep it short and sweet, letting him know that this isn't some fling but that his friendship means everything to me and I could never jeopardize that. I just need to know if there's a chance for more, or if I need to find a way to move on once and for all.

He did mention flowers. Maybe it would be better to grab the small hand-picked flowers and letter before anyone can see it and buy a big bouquet tonight. I can leave it tomorrow.

"Caleb?" Chuck says while putting one hand on my shoulder. "Are you sure you're ready for this? You look a little worried."

"Sorry, I was thinking about something else. I'm good to go." I pat his shoulder in response and catch Matt looking almost pointedly away from us.

He's not really doing anything at the moment so I must have upset him by making it obvious my thoughts were scattered. I need to focus on the mare so I don't make a beginner mistake.

"If you're sure." Chuck gives me a meaningful look. It's one that I'm used to by now. There's worry and trepidation along with support. I've seen variations of it from all five brothers while recovering.

"I'm sure," I say, seeing Matt take a deep breath out of the corner of my eye. He looks so tightly wound that I just want to make whatever is bothering him go away.

But focusing on him won't help us right now as Bryant leads the tan mare out to the corral.

"How'd she do getting the saddle on?" Chuck asks as he chews his toothpick, going over to the fence.

"Good."

I used to think that Bryant didn't talk much because crowds overwhelmed him, kind of like Jax. But it didn't take long for me to see that he's a man of few words just about everywhere. I can recall only a couple of instances since I moved to Greenstone where he's elaborated on anything. So I take his response as meaning it wasn't a disaster and no one got kicked.

"You guys got this handled?" he asks, looking at each of us in turn.

We're practically the same age, but I feel like I should raise my hand and wait to be called on before I answer his question. Instead, I nod while his brothers say, "Yep."

"Will you latch the gate on your way out?" Chuck asks.

Bryant grunts an affirmative response and turns to leave us, giving Matt the reins.

I take a few steps until I'm an arm's length from the horse and let her sniff me. My fingers rub her velvety nose when I hear a *clang* followed by a low curse behind me.

"Are you okay?" Matt calls out, staying put, while Chuck rushes towards whatever's going on.

Keeping my movements slow so I don't spook her shortly before I ride her, I turn around to see Bryant on his hands and knees with the gate closed in front of him.

"Fucking mud," Bryant growls, waving off Chuck. "I'm fine, I just slipped shutting the damn gate."

"Are you sure?" Chuck asks, still offering a hand.

Bryant kneels in the mud and even though his back is to us, I can picture the scowl on his face because the middle sibling takes a step back and holds up both hands in surrender.

A few grumbles later, he's through the gate and stomping towards the house, shaking off mud as he goes.

"Don't you dare laugh just yet," Matt warns, drawing my attention to Chuck who is now turning red from holding back said laughter.

"Did you see how caked he was?" he asks in a tight voice. "Even his face was covered."

"Stop, he'll hear you and then he'll be even crankier."

Chuck fights to keep his mirth contained now that he knows his brother is okay.

"Let's get this show on the road," I say, trying to distract both of them because the more Matt points out Chuck's need to laugh, the harder it is for him to not burst out in his trademark cackle that everyone will hear, including Bryant.

I must not be paying attention as I turn around because the next thing I know, I'm slipping on the mud, leaning hard to the left so I don't slide right into the mare. Fortunately, I avoid hitting her.

Unfortunately, I managed to slam into Matt's feet, taking him with me. He lets go of the reins and the horse startles, rearing back. Both of us automatically curl into a ball to protect ourselves and in the rush, we end up wound together with one of my arms at his back to pull him closer as his hand presses my helmet under his shoulder, shielding my head as best he can.

With my heart pounding with the adrenaline rush, one thought consumes me:

Even in an emergency, we're drawn together like magnets.

Chapter 27
Matt

Keep him safe. Keep him safe. Keep him safe.

Nothing else matters except making sure Caleb is okay.

"I've got her," Chuck calls, slightly out of breath somewhere else in the corral with the mare.

Maybe it's because I feel like I'm about to lose Caleb to my brother, but I hold on for an extra second or two. For some reason, so does he.

"Are you alright?" I ask, releasing the grip on his helmet but placing that hand on his shoulder as he loosens the arm he has thrown over my side.

"Yeah, just a klutz, that's all. How are you?"

"How's your head?"

"I'm alright, really." His eyes are soft and kind. "You didn't answer my question."

"Fine, just worried." Now that I think about how my own body feels, I'm pretty sure I'll have a nice bruise on my left hip. I don't really remember my own fall.

I vividly remember his, though.

It wasn't in slow motion like the accident. It was as if I needed to catalog every tiny detail of him going down. Whatever my body went through, I don't know. All I could focus on was the resounding *not again* in my head spurring me into whatever action I took to try to break his fall.

Looking at both of us in the mud, I don't think I was very successful. However, besides being filthy, we seem to be okay.

"Neither of you got kicked, right? She seemed to shift to the side and back from my view," Chuck comments as he approaches and we fully separate.

"Nope, the worst is a bruised ego, I think," Caleb replies, taking the hand Chuck offers him and standing. "But it's nothing that I won't get over."

I avoid watching more of their interaction because I can hear the smile in his voice. When I'm almost standing, a familiar hand is at the small of my back, making sure I'm steady.

"Whoa there, don't slip."

My footing is solid, but I don't say that because I want Caleb's hand to stay right where it is.

"Thanks," I mutter, glancing at Chuck who is looking us over.

"Well, I think getting on this little lady will have to wait." He tips his head towards the horse in question.

Her reins are wrapped around the fence making up the corral and she looks no worse for wear. I'm about to go over and check on her when my brother keeps talking, which is something he does when he's worried about someone, or just anxious in general.

"Let me know if you need something for any aches or cuts," he says. It's not like he needs to remind me he practically has a pharmacy in his bathroom keeping us all in one piece. "You two better get in the house and clean up before that mud dries. It's a lot faster to clean it off now, I promise."

Caleb's eyebrows raise. "And you're the expert on mud around here?"

"Don't you forget it," he says, reaching into his pocket and popping a toothpick into his mouth.

"Chuck, you didn't swallow a toothpick or anything did you?" I ask.

He laughs. "No, little brother, I spit it out so I wouldn't be impaled like a good scout."

"You were never a scout," I mumble. It's an automatic reaction whenever he or Jax make a scout reference.

"Go inside and get clean," he says, waving us off. "I'll let her run around in here for a bit with the saddle on."

"Thanks," I say, leaving the corral with Caleb at my side.

He takes over latching the gate closed and says, "I should head home."

"Don't be ridiculous, your truck will be wrecked inside with this much mud."

"I have a blanket I can put down," he counters.

"Just come inside and you can put on something of mine," I say, liking the idea of him wearing my things far too much.

"You want me to come up to your room?" For some reason, he looks nervous as he rubs behind one ear, finding mud.

"Yeah, you can use my bathroom, or the one across the hall." I'm able to say it like it's no big deal.

"Really, I can be home quickly—"

"Cay," I say, interrupting him. "Is there a reason you don't want to come in?"

He swallows hard. "No."

"Alright, then stop being so weird, let's go."

"Okay."

He stays half a step behind and I can't stand whatever is going on. On a whim for how to get him out of this funk, I look back at him and say, "Race ya. Whoever steps foot inside the house first wins."

"What does the winner get?"

"The winner gets dough for a dozen of Avery's oatmeal chocolate chunk cookies and the loser has to sneak into Jax's house to steal it from the freezer."

"Deal," he says, taking off a split second before me.

It's awkward as hell to run in muddy cowboy boots, but we're both laughing as we slip and slide our way to the main house, jumping on one foot, then the other, as we pull off our boots on the porch. We practically tumble through the door, breathing heavily.

"Tie?" he asks, his cheeks rosy.

"Tie."

Tommy's laughter greets us while he takes in the sight of us. "Do I get to know what happened now?"

Hmmm, I'm guessing he saw Bryant come in a minute ago and I can't imagine he was forthcoming with details with how grumpy his slip made him.

"We attempted to get my ass in the saddle," Caleb explains, pushing his curls off his forehead as I put my hat, which somehow was spared getting filthy, on a hook. "As you might have guessed by my appearance, I didn't make it."

The two of us are about to burst into laughter, but my brother rushes over.

"Shit, are you okay?"

Immediately, I swat Tommy away so Caleb doesn't feel smothered or embarrassed. I just got him laughing after being so odd outside.

"He never got a boot in the stirrup, he's okay," I explain. "We had a helmet on him the whole time, too."

Unfortunately, Tommy doesn't seem convinced that everything is alright and he gives us both a stern look. "Did the doctor give the okay for him to ride a horse that has only recently gotten used to wearing a saddle?"

"I was cleared to ride." There's a stubborn set to Caleb's jaw as he says it, so I instantly know what he's been up to.

And I'm already fuming.

"Are you saying you weren't, in fact, cleared for *all* styles of riding? Because that's what you've been inferring."

Chapter 28
Caleb

All I can do right now is shut my damn mouth because I won't lie to his face.

Have I been purposefully omitting details? For sure.

Have I been lying? Technically no.

Which isn't great, I know. There's no excuse.

So, I'm not surprised at everything I see on Matt's face. Each emotion passes so rapidly that they'd be hard for most people to recognize. But not me. First, there's concern, then surprise, followed by skepticism which morphs right into anger. There's a moment of hope that he's not going to be as mad as I think because he looks at me with pure sympathy. But that switches to sadness, frustration, and settles into good old fashioned pissed off before he speaks.

"What the fuck are you trying to do? Do you want to go back to the hospital for another month?" He's steaming mad now. "I was there with you, and I'm not going to let you do something bone-headed just because you're bored or think you have something to prove to the cowboys traveling with the rodeo."

He takes a breath, his face turning red from all his emotions bubbling over, and I take advantage of the break.

"And what, I wasn't there? I was the one in the goddamn bed, hooked up to monitors, getting my ass wiped by nurses while in a neck brace and two casts," I say, breathing hard and matching the anger radiating off of him from my stupid risk. "Do you have *any* idea what it was like to be riding a bull one minute and—"

The intensity in his gaze falters as my words do.

"Cay," his voice is gentler and his hand reaches towards me before falling back at his side. I ignore the small sting that comes with the action.

Some of the fight deflates in me.

I know I was being an idiot.

"It wasn't the same as living through it, I know. But I was there and saw what you went through."

"Except you got to go home to your own bed any time you wanted." He winces almost imperceptibly. "You got to wear your own clothes, shower without help, hell, you could wear your damn cologne every day."

Cologne that lingered long after he left the room.

"Cay," he tries again, but apparently, I'm on a bit of a roll now.

"You were there for me like no one has ever been. Period." I never want him to think he didn't do enough. If anything, he's gone above and beyond. "But that's not the same, Matt. When you look in the mirror, you don't see the scars from that nightmare. You aren't reminded every god damn day that your short-term memory has become a fucking liability. I finally get to settle down in a small town of my choosing and I can't even remember the name of the person who has been my cashier at the grocery store for the last month. So excuse me for wanting to feel alive again for the first time in months. For doing the one thing that granted me my freedom ten years ago. Something I'm damn good at. Something that I don't have to work for."

I take a deep breath and release it in a long sigh. He's still pissed at me, but I think he's less likely to lay into me some more. For now. I'm sure we're not done with this topic.

"I'll do better," I say, looking for Tommy so he knows I'm not trying to sabotage anything, but he's not in the entryway anymore. *When did he leave?*

"No one needs you to do anything other than to finish healing." He holds up one hand to stop me from cutting him off, which is smart since apparently my knee-jerk response right now is to be petulant and tell him I'm healed enough or that I won't fall out of the saddle. "You don't have to prove anything to anyone here."

It would be so easy to tell him I'm not trying to *prove* anything, but I'm not lying, so I just say, "Thanks."

"Is there anything else you need to let your emergency contact know about?" he asks, lightening the mood a bit.

"No, I promise you know the rest."

"Good," he says. Then he nods at the staircase in front of us. "Let's get cleaned up. You can wear my clothes, come o n."

I follow him up the stairs and stop at the top, knowing exactly what's in front of his door. There's no getting out of this without making it into a bigger deal than it needs to be.

Who am I kidding? It's a huge deal.

My palms are getting slicker with sweat the closer we get to the turn at the end of the hallway. Then he stops dead in his tracks, the muscles in his jaw working overtime.

He knows what this is, there's no way he forgot the advice he gave me.

Fuck, this is such a disaster. I'm about to turn around, take the stairs two at a time, and run to my truck, mud be damned, when he looks up at the ceiling and grits out a, "Thanks," between clenched teeth.

I'm so shocked by his overall demeanor that I don't think twice when I ask, "What?"

He clears his throat, still tense, as he gestures stiffly to his door. "For the thank you flowers. I assume you're telling him today?"

Thank you flowers?

"What?" I ask again.

He sighs, still looking at the damn ceiling like the flowers have offended him.

Fuck, I never could have imagined this going so terribly.

"You didn't have to get me something, too," he says, his voice hoarse with emotion.

"What?" My mind races as I try to figure out what he thinks is going on.

He finally looks at me, his blue eyes sad and resigned. "They'll look amazing on Gertrude."

I cough out an astonished laugh. "You think *Chuck's* door has something?"

He goes quiet as his chest rises and falls.

"Matt," I say, finding more bravery than I've ever needed to summon while riding the most formidable bull. "No one else has anything. At least nothing from me."

He shifts from one foot to the other, watching me. I stay still, letting him work past whatever he was thinking. Finally, he peeks down at the flowers once more and then stares.

"I didn't see the note. I looked away too quickly," he whispers.

Hope that I haven't felt since the hospital when I woke up with his hand in mine blooms in my chest. Trying to not let my emotions get carried away, I gesture towards the note even though he's not looking at me. "You should read it."

That seems to be enough to get him to take those few steps to his door and pick it up, almost reverently. I can barely hear him carefully tearing open the envelope with the sound of my heartbeat whooshing in my ears.

Finally, he opens the note and starts reading.

And I know, without a doubt, everything is about to change, for better or worse.

Chapter 29
Matt

My door.

My name.

Not Chuck's.

This isn't a thank you note in my hands. The flowers weren't part of a larger bouquet as another way to say thank you for giving him advice on how to tell my brother his feelings.

Feelings he doesn't have for Chuck.

Feelings he has for me.

Feelings he's had for me for a while, according to what he's written.

I feel frozen in place, my mind and heart trying to catch up with what's in front of me.

"Why didn't you say anything before now?" I ask, my eyes glued to the note, trying to memorize every word, like I'm afraid it's going to disappear.

His chuckle rumbles in his chest. "I think I finally did that first night in the hospital."

I glance at him, watching him rub the back of his neck.

"Well, yeah, you did then, but not when you were...yourself. I assumed it was just the meds talking."

"And I assumed you'd say something if you felt anything."

"I—" I pause.

"Why didn't you come to the auction?" he blurts out.

"Why'd you sign up for the auction?" I counter, finally giving voice to that question from weeks ago.

"I wanted to do something for this place that has been your home. To show that I could be a positive, upstanding citizen. Someone who gives back just a fraction of what you do." He says it like it should have been obvious.

"I was jealous," I say, responding to his question. "I didn't want to see you on a date. Even a group date raising funds for better vet equipment."

"I wanted you in the audience and I wanted you to win the bid for me."

Suddenly, there's too much space between us and I let the note flutter to the ground next to the wildflowers. The dam holding back years' worth of feelings breaks, flooding me with the need to finally close that distance, mud be damned.

The three strides it takes to reach him gives Caleb enough time to know my intentions. His eyes blaze with intensity and he leans in, making those last few inches disappear. One hand slips around the back of his neck so I can finally bury my fingers in his curls while the other grabs his hip, my grip tight and squelching in the mud stuck to it, as his arm wraps around my waist.

The moment our lips touch, I'm done for. I know I've been his for so much longer than I ever realized, because nothing has ever felt like this. For once, I'm not overthinking a damn thing. I'm exactly where I've dreamt of being for years, and it's heaven.

His lips respond to mine and follow my lead, moving in rhythm together, as one of his hands anchors itself on the side of my neck, his thumb rubbing lazy circles against my jaw. When I tug ever-so-slightly on his hair, he tips his head back and opens his mouth, letting my tongue dive in to meet his. We groan the moment we taste each other, like we've both been denying ourselves for far too long. Fuck, can you describe someone's mouth as minty and perfect?

His beard might be scratchier than I imagined, but I'm obsessed with the feeling. Already picturing the redness it will leave behind long after we're done kissing.

Applying the slightest pressure at his hip, his body is fully flush against mine. His toned muscles press into me and I feel his cock hardening.

Again, the feeling of too much between us strikes and I'm walking backwards with him in-step with me. His hand stops roaming my back to turn the knob and I release him long enough to quickly toss the bouquet and note far enough into the room so we won't crush them.

I practically pounce on him inside my bedroom, pressing his back against the door to latch it shut and searching his eyes for consent as my fingers reach for the bottom of his shirt. What I get is so much better because he whispers the word, "Please."

Suddenly, he grabs my wrist and I worry he needs to think about something. "Wait, this is going to be hell to clean up," he says breathlessly.

He's right, there's already going to be a bunch of mud on my door from the back of his shirt alone. He glances at the door to my bathroom and we both move, unable to stop our kisses as we go. I raise the T-shirt up and over his head just as we cross the threshold, throwing it in the general direction of the hamper. My fingers explore his chest while my mouth slowly kisses, nips, and licks his throat.

God, seeing this man's bare torso is nothing compared to touching it. I'm addicted to feeling him take in a sharp breath when my fingers pass over the trail of dark hair that disappears into his jeans or when my thumb brushes his nipple all while he's kissing me senseless. Even with his chest here just for me, I'm unable to resist tangling my fingers in his hair. I must be making up for all the times I wished I could do this.

Finally, I lean down and take his nipple into my mouth and he gasps. I'm pleasantly surprised that he's so sensitive here because it takes a significant tug for me to have any reaction with nipple play. When I flick the bud with my tongue, both of his hands grip the sides of my head, keeping me right there.

He jerks his hips forward and, as I keep up my ministrations, my free hand glides across his abs until I feel his trail. I'm on the verge of becoming painfully hard and will need to stroke myself to provide a little relief, but then I reach his buckle. The one I've seen him wear ever since I first watched him ride.

The cold of the metal is a sharp contrast to the heat coming from his skin. I feel around and am able to unbuckle it single-handily and pop open the button to his jeans. A small voice in the back of my mind tries to tell me that I might be terrible at this since I haven't been with a guy before. But something about being with Caleb Harlow has me telling that little cloud of doubt to go fuck itself, because I know this man and I know what feels amazing to me and we can start there.

With that thought, I drop to my knees.

Chapter 30
Caleb

Somehow, I had the coherent thought to give Matt the green light, but now he's kneeling before me, about to take my pants off, while he's fully dressed. I think every time I've gotten enough wits about me to unfasten the top buttons of his flannel shirt and pull it over his head, he goes and does something that feels fucking amazing.

"Hang on," I pant, worrying that this is going to be over for me shortly with how zeroed-in he is on my pleasure. He glances up at me with a slight frown. "You have far too much on if we're going to shower."

"Why Caleb," he says with a cocky grin, "are you in a hurry to get me naked? The water isn't even running."

"Abso-fucking-lutely," I reply, stepping away from him and turning on the shower. When I'm facing him again, he's still wearing that same grin, but he's standing which means he's just as ready as I am to remove his layers. "It's time for you to lose the shirt so I can touch you."

He reaches up and undoes the top two buttons, eyes never leaving mine, making it hard to think again. Then he grips the back collar of his shirt, giving it a sharp tug. Because he hunches over to easily remove the shirt, I get a great view of his back, briefly watching the muscles ripple. A wave of his cologne wafts through the air and by the time he's straightened up, my mouth is on his neck and my hands caress his shoulders before moving down his chest. As I feel his pecs for the first time, he snakes his hand to my hair, tipping my head back and claiming my lips with his like he's been doing this for years. He's solid muscle with a little padding on top from a lifetime on this ranch, his skin smooth and unmarred by recent scars like mine.

He devours the whimper that tries to escape me when his free arm pulls us tight together at the waist and he rocks against me with his bulge. My partially open fly catches on his buckle and he makes a frustrated sound in the back of his throat.

"Off," he demands, grabbing his belt with one hand and maneuvering the whole thing off in a few sure movements.

As much as I loathe taking my hands off of him, I'm desperate for what's next. With his mouth back on me and his tongue against mine once more, I finish unzipping my pants and shove them down so they fall around my ankles. He's already unbuttoned his jeans, but I push his hand away and slowly lower the zipper.

He cups my face, kissing me harder, as my fingers feel the outline of his shaft. Even though I'm still in my boxer briefs, which are feeling far too tight, I hook my thumbs in the waistband of his, pushing everything down his hips, circling to the front to free him. He keeps me locked in his kisses as we step out of our pants and then I feel his tip touch on my lower abdomen.

He takes in a sharp breath and we both look down at where his precum has left a small spot just above the waistband of my tented underwear. I take him in my hand, feeling his girth for the first time and making him moan. He's thicker than I imagined, but nothing I can't wrap my lips around. Giving him one pump though is all I get before he's removing my final article of clothing and getting us under the water.

"I'm clean," he says, his voice huskier than I've ever heard before.

"Same."

He chuckles and then nips at my earlobe before saying, "Oh I know."

Of course he does, he's seen all my test results from the hospital.

The next thing I know my back's against the wall with his hand cushioning my head and then he's grinding against me, our dicks slippery from the shower.

"Fuck that feels good," I say into his hair as he sucks on my neck, likely leaving a mark that I'll be staring at for hours later just to remind myself this wasn't a dream. He's probably going to have scratches on his back from the way I'm holding on every time my knees get weak. We'll both leave this shower with marks.

When I reach between us, he joins me and we curse as our hands grab our thrusting dicks together, heightening the pressure. That tingling feeling builds deep inside of me and the pleasure almost becomes too much.

"You have to slow down if you don't want me—"

"Don't fight it, cowboy," he says, cutting me off then running our hands over my sensitive head.

It's like I'm getting my first hand job because my sack tightens and that's all the warning I get before my cum spurts onto Matt's abs, the sight alone almost enough to get me hard again.

Before I can catch my breath fully, I shift so it's only me pumping him, twisting my wrist to cover his head on each stroke. I drop the hand that was digging into his back moments ago to cradle his balls.

His kisses are almost bruising as he gets closer to his own climax. With his free hand braced against the wall, he pulls back, panting, and looks down at how I'm working him, faster and faster. His mouth falls open and he grunts as he comes between my fingers, everything sticky and hot. Then he slumps against me, spent and breathing hard. His weight is soothing and I wrap my arms around him, letting the water clean my fingers.

After a moment, he laughs.

My mind starts spinning with what could have gone wrong and before I can come up with any ideas, he gives me a long, languid kiss.

"That is *not* how I expected things to go when we raced to the front door."

A relieved laugh breaks free and I wrap my arms around him while the water beats down on his back. "Fuck, me neither."

He nuzzles his face into the crook of my neck and we just stay here, completely naked, having just come on each other, feeling content. The nuzzling turns into kissing as he works his way to my jaw, nipping once, which startles me. He's clearly expecting my reaction though because he's swallowing the sound with a kiss that seems like it's sealing something between us.

At least I hope so.

His teeth tug my lower lip before he takes a step back. "Turn around."

I raise an eyebrow at him as I follow his instructions. "Someone's bossy since he got some flowers."

"Are you complaining, cowboy?" he asks, pressing himself against me and holding me in place with one arm wrapped around my waist, but not dropping lower.

My head falls back on its own accord with him holding me like this. "No, chef."

A rumble of approval comes from his chest as his dick twitches against my ass.

Best fucking shower ever.

Chapter 31
Matt

Holy shit.

My best friend and I just did *that*.

We might have set a speed record, but it seems like we've both had some pent-up attraction building for quite some time. We'll have plenty of opportunities to draw things out in the future though.

Or sneak away for a quickie.

Reluctantly, I pull away from Caleb, being conscientious to keep my hand on his washboard abs and not lower. I know that his belt got muddy and I want to make sure it's not damaged because I was greedy and it wasn't cleaned off soon enough.

He tries to turn around but I make a tutting sound while I grab my shampoo, squirting some into my palm.

"What are you doing back there?"

Instead of answering his question, I mutter, "Relax, Cay, I've got you."

When my lathered up fingers begin massaging his scalp, he lets out a soft moan. Each sound I've been able to elicit from him makes it feel like he's mine.

I know we'll have to talk about what we're doing and how to make sure our feelings don't affect where he ends up. Especially anything that could make him feel the need to leave Greenstone.

Just the thought of him leaving is something that could easily send me into a panic. I shove it deep down because, like an absolute fool, I want him to stay. My brothers would never object to having him here permanently.

But that's getting too far ahead of things. So far, I've gotten a note, flowers, and one damn sexy shower.

You've never had a relationship last more than seven months.

My jaw clenches at the invasive thought. It's true, sure. But for the last few years, I was clearly interested in someone I thought was unobtainable, so that has to be part of the reason nothing worked.

Right?

That stupid tightness in my chest tries to start and I put all my focus on how it feels to shift Caleb so I can rinse his hair. The sound the water makes as it drips off his body. The way the shampoo runs from his hair, over his necklace, down his toned back, and onto his ass.

I give myself a moment to appreciate how good it looks, especially when he shifts his weight to his other foot and I get to see his muscles flex and relax.

"My turn," he says, looking back at me and making small circles with his index finger so I'll turn around myself.

"I'm not the only bossy one, it seems."

"You get to take care of me, and I get to do the same," he says, squirting product into his hands then rubbing them together. "It's only fair."

His fingers massage my scalp in slow, sure strokes, and my eyes flutter closed.

When was the last time someone other than Courtney, who cuts my hair, did this? Come to think of it, I'm not sure the last person I did this for. Something in the moment just felt right with Caleb, though. This is a different level of intimacy than I'm used to and recognizing that has my chest tightening.

"Relax, Matt," he whispers, kissing my shoulder and running his sudsy hands down my biceps.

I force my mind to focus on what he's doing and how good it feels. I remind myself of his note and that he's choosing me. He's not here because he feels bad for the youngest Landen brother for whatever reason my fucked up brain can come up with. He's here because he took a risk and told me how he feels.

My head can't fight against the evidence I have in the next room and it's like a balloon of tension deflates, allowing me to relax and enjoy what's happening.

"There you go. Head back now."

I listen, letting the water and his fingertips rinse my hair.

When he's done, I take over once more, working my conditioner into his hair. He's going to smell like my products and he'll be wearing my clothes soon. I can't fucking wait.

"Leave it in while I do yours," he says when I go to rinse it out. "Otherwise, my hair will be frizzy without product when it dries."

I frown, unsure how I missed that at the hospital. I think back on what the nurses did when he'd need sponge baths, but most of the time, I'd run errands or read over notes and emails to summarize for him. I didn't set up his bathroom, either, that was Chuck since he's the one who we go to if we need medicine. The guy is a walking dispensary.

Caleb's hands work the conditioner into the ends of my shorter hair. "You look like you're working out a puzzle."

"I never noticed you have hair products."

He fights back a smile.

"Is that something you needed to know about me?"

I think on that as he turns me around and has me tip my head back so he can rinse the conditioner out of my hair.

"It seems weird that I hadn't, especially after these past few months."

He chuckles. "Well, now you know."

I make a mental note to check what he keeps in his bathroom cabinet so I can keep some here. There's no way we aren't having future showers together now.

We opt for lathering and applying our own body wash, so we don't spend the next hour in here, and I step out first, drying myself just enough so I don't leave a lake in front of the closet while I grab him a towel.

"Damn this is soft," he says, starting with his face and hair.

"Wait until you feel my sheets," I say, grinning.

"Fuck, we're never going to leave your room," he groans.

I laugh. "Knowing my brothers will be calling if we're gone too long is motivation to keep things short this time."

"Fair point."

Wrapping my towel around my waist, I get things out of my cabinet that I normally use, like my deodorant, SPF face lotion, and cologne, assuming that Caleb will want them, too.

"Dive in. Want me to see if Chuck has something for your hair? If anyone has something, it would be him." I'm grateful that there's no stab of jealousy talking to Caleb about my brother. The look on his face when I told him I thought Chuck was getting the note was enough to squash that thought.

"Nah, I'm good. I just didn't rinse everything out of my hair," he explains.

"Alright."

And because I can, I grab his chin then give him a long, open-mouthed kiss.

Chapter 32
Caleb

I could kiss this man all fucking day.

As he uses the toiletries he set out, I look around, noticing that nothing is sitting on the counters. Not even a toothbrush or a glass. The bathroom has a decent amount of storage with cabinets, drawers, and even a closet, but it seems that nothing has been updated in here besides the shower features. It kind of feels like a kid's bathroom, but with everything tucked away.

I've been in his room before and don't think anything has ever been cluttered.

"Do you always keep things off the counters?"

He pauses while rubbing lotion on his face and blinks a couple of times. "I guess so."

The kitchen is always neat, but it's a shared space. His truck, on the other hand, is usually a little messy. Nothing major, but it's not pristine like he keeps spaces in the house. Especially looking out the open door into his room. Beyond a couple of photos on his dresser and a clock and a book next to his bed, there's *nothing* out.

"I hadn't realized just how clean you keep things, you must lose your mind when you're at my place with all the things I have sitting out."

He works his jaw and looks down at the counter while he thinks. I give him time, peek at one hell of a hickey that a flannel shirt collar *might* cover, and use everything except his cologne. Is it tempting to use his cologne though? Yes. But now, I have something better than a spritz from a bottle. I can wrap myself around the man himself and smell like him all day.

"I don't like being messy," he begins, pausing as he grips the counter and frowns. His Adam's apple bobs once while he swallows before speaking again. "I've never wanted to be a burden."

My heart breaks for him.

Who would ever see him as a burden?

Who made him feel like he might be one?

I put my hand on his bare lower back, lending silent support as he finds his words.

"So I've kept things like this for as long as I can remember. Mary says it's from my mom leaving." He huffs out a breath, rolling his eyes. "A lot of what I talked with Mary about over the years seemed to stem from her abandoning us."

"Do you feel like you're a burden?" I ask, rubbing small circles against his skin.

"I know I'm not, but..." He trails off.

I wait, still rubbing those little circles, hoping to provide support.

"I know she didn't leave because of me. It still doesn't change the fact that she was fine staying until the fifth son was old enough to add enough stress and chaos to life at the ranch. But did I feel like it was my fault and that I did something wrong? Of course I did. And then when Dad...when he died, she was 'willing' to take me," he says, releasing the counter to make air quotes. "The woman who had practically become a stranger to all five of us. God, I didn't want to go.

"Jax asked me if I wanted to stay here with them one time." He takes a deep breath and faces me, my hand sliding to his hip, his eyes shining with emotion as he remembers. "It was at a dinner and all four of them were staring at me while pretending to *not* be staring at me. And I froze up. I didn't want to fucking move away from my home, my family, horse, my entire way of life, to live with someone who sent me a card on my birthday and whose calls I rarely answered. But how could I ask them to become my guardians?"

Running his hand through his hair, he shakes his head. "Sorry, I don't know where all this is coming from."

"There's nothing to be sorry for. I asked, and anything you're willing to share, I want to hear." I lean forward and give his cheek a kiss.

He grabs the back of my neck and keeps me near, our chests close to touching as he presses our foreheads together. I want to fully wrap him in my arms, but this is all so new and even though we know a lot about each other, this isn't something he talks about. Ever. And just because we took one huge step doesn't mean there aren't topics that shouldn't be pushed.

I'm not sure how long we stand like this, but nothing feels forced or off. It feels like everything could be falling into place in its own time.

"Thank you," he says, his voice quiet but calm.

"There's nothing to thank me for. I'm here for you."

Those soft lips of his brush against mine and then he steps back and looks down at the floor.

"Where'd your pants—found them." Matt scoops up my jeans and gently removes my belt from the loops. He seems worried about it as he examines it, which is sweet.

"I replace the leather fairly often, so I really don't mind if that's damaged," I tell him. His brow relaxes a little.

"Nothing's that bad," he says, sounding relieved.

"You're kind of adorable, you know that?" I tease, leaning against the counter.

"I think ranchers are supposed to be rugged," he says.

"Ruggedly adorable," I amend.

He rolls his eyes and then proceeds to get the dirt off the belt and the buckle. While he does that, I shake out our clothes into the tub, but when I get to our pants, I pull out our phones and see a few missed messages from Cooper. I almost set my phone aside, assuming that he's wanting to know about the sparkling water ad and if he should book it. I really don't care about that potential endorsement, especially since I like this little bubble away from the stress of life in the spotlight.

Not wanting to be rude and ignore him, I unlock my screen and scan what he sent. It isn't about an endorsement.

"Hey, Cooper was able to grab me two tickets to the rodeo tomorrow. It's only an hour away. Want to go?" I ask, not thinking twice about inviting Matt.

"Yeah, what time does it start?" He looks over his shoulder at me, pausing his work carefully picking dirt out of one spot of my buckle.

Damn, he's sexy.

Especially with a few fresh scratches on his back.

"Gates open at two."

He nods and pulls a washcloth out of a drawer to dry my buckle. "We could grab dinner after, before heading back."

It feels like we might have stumbled on a real date sooner than I would have expected. Maybe this is just...happening.

"Sounds good," I say, laying our pants out in the tub so there isn't mud on his floor, excited and hopeful for what's to come.

Chapter 33
Matt

Am I picking out one of my smaller shirts so it's not loose on Caleb?

Absolutely.

He probably has more muscles than I do, but he's a little shorter than me with a slimmer frame.

"These pants are going to look pornographic with how low they'll sit," he says, holding out the gray joggers that are one size too big, and I can already imagine what they'll look like.

"I'll help you cinch the waist extra tight," I offer with a wink, then open my underwear drawer and pull out two pairs before getting socks.

"Tommy's might fit me better, or even Chuck's."

I hear the teasing in his voice, but I still shoot him a glare. He just laughs.

"Want to stay in for the rest of the evening?"

"Yeah, unless there's something outside we didn't do."

I shake my head in response, handing him the rest of the clothes. Tugging him closer by the towel wrapped around his waist, I kiss him. It's quick, only a peck on the lips, enough to remind me that it's okay to do. It's like part of me is worried if we go too long without something, he'll change his mind.

He grumbles something under his breath while I get my underwear on, tossing the rest of my clothes on the bed and letting my towel drop on the floor.

"What was that?"

"I said that they should come in twos."

Frowning, I try to figure out what he's talking about.

"Kisses," he says. "You shouldn't be allowed to just come up and kiss me once. There should always be at least two."

I can't hold back my smile. "Is that right?"

"Yes," he replies matter-of-factly while I saunter over to him.

"Well, I wouldn't want to break any rules."

I pull him close with his towel once more. I run both hands over his abs, up to his pecs, and then slowly on his shoulders. One finger traces his necklace for a few seconds, and I watch his skin pebble with goosebumps. Finally, I slip my hands up so I'm cradling his face. His breathing is heavy by the time I'm pressed against him and he's getting hard even before our lips touch.

This time, the kiss is slow and thorough. I'm careful to not break it off until our tongues are tangled together and I've drawn out a whimper from him. Only then do I come in for one more kiss, tilting his head back and thrusting my tongue in deep. His moan vibrates against my skin. But I pull away and nudge his nose with mine.

"That was two," I say with a smirk.

His hooded eyes slowly open wide with shock as his jaw drops. "You're a dick."

I shrug. "A dick you like."

He tosses the sweats at my face, mumbling, "Shut up."

We laugh as we get dressed and it feels normal. I've always felt like the little kid of the family who has to ask permission for everything. It wasn't *that* long ago that I was a minor, I suppose. But besides getting myself a "grown-up" bed in here a few years ago and upgrading our kitchen equipment, I haven't really made any changes to this entire house. Not that I need to, everything is what we need. As much as I crave a space to make my own, I want *this*.

Someone to share my life with.

Someone who gets me.

Someone who sees more in me than I do most days.

As I look at Caleb in this space, I can see how easy it would be to have him here. Right in this room with me, carving out our own little life. Sure, it'd be nice to have a house to ourselves, but this would work. He'd blend right into our little family if he wanted to.

And I hope he does.

My thoughts are interrupted by my phone buzzing on the bathroom counter.

"I suppose it's time to return to the real world," I say absentmindedly.

"Yeah, I guess so."

A message from Chuck comes through.

"There's a German forklift competition on soon. Chuck's making popcorn and wants to know if we're in," I call out to Caleb.

"A what?"

Chuckling, I bring our phones out along with a basket of our dirty clothes. "A German forklift competition. It's exactly what it sounds like. Forklift operators go through a series of challenges, stacking different things without them toppling over in a timed race."

"Is this anything like the roller skating limbo competition we watched not that long ago?"

"Well, this one is forklifts."

"And it's in German," he states.

"Yep."

He looks at me, confused. "Have I missed the part where you all know German?"

"Nope," I say. "Not one of us speaks it, but the announcers are ridiculously enthusiastic and make it sound like the most exciting sport of all time and Chuck gets really into it. Just wait until the duct tape competition airs in Germany and he can get his hands on that."

"Alright, I'm sold."

"For the duct tape competition or the forklift?"

"Do I have to choose?"

I hold the basket against my hip with one hand and clap him on the back with the other. "That's the spirit."

And with that, we leave my room, something shifting. It's nothing big, but noticeable. A little more space between us while we walk to the washing machine. Not as much as usual, but still something.

"Would you mind grabbing a pint glass and bringing it up so I can put my flowers in it?" I ask. "I'll get these in the wash."

"Of course," he says, heading down the steps.

I try not to read into it.

He left me pretty fast, even though I asked him to.

But it's to bring up something so the flowers he brought me don't die.

It's not like I can't do laundry by myself.

Oh fuck, I have to get my head on right or I'm going to overanalyze every damn thing.

Chapter 34
Caleb

My alarm goes off for the fourth time. It's time to finally sit up, rub the sleep from my eyes, and stop hitting the snooze button.

Tossing my covers to the side, I put on my slippers, because these floors are damn cold in the mornings, and walk over to open the shades on my bedroom window. It's nothing like the view from the ranch, but I can see a little bit of the mountains from this room, which I like.

It's still dark outside as I head to the bathroom. The sun should be rising soon, and I like keeping similar hours to the Landens.

One in particular.

When I look in the mirror, I angle my head so I can better see the mark Matt left on my neck yesterday.

God, I can still feel his touch.

And I can still hear Chuck's worried tone when he asked if I got that mark during the fall in the corral. It took just about everything in my power to not look at Matt. We hadn't talked about what we are at that point.

Still haven't.

But I did get one hell of a kiss goodnight at my truck. Matt had me pressed against the driver's door and weak in the knees like I was a damn teenager again within a few seconds. If I wasn't so unsure if he wanted his brothers to know about the shift between us, I would have asked him to come home with me.

Before that, the three of us sat on the main couch and eventually Bryant joined us, taking one of the recliners. We were all on our feet screaming by the end of the last round because the final contestant was about to beat the leader's time by a full minute. Did we all jump around like maniacs when he won? Yep, even Bryant.

These guys make me feel right at home. Kind of like I've found my family, the one that means more than any blood relation ever could.

And with everything that's happened with Matt in the last twenty-four hours...

I don't know if I should be excited or scared shitless that I'll screw things up with him and lose everything, or if this is the start of having *everything*.

Any time I'm not with Matt, I'll probably waffle between excited and scared shitless.

As I'm driving to the ranch, the sun is just starting to rise, adding soft colors to the sky. I wonder what the chance is that I might be driving into town less and less, maybe even spending nights in Matt's bed.

I'm definitely getting ahead of myself.

We made out yesterday and had one hell of a shower. We didn't declare our undying love for each other.

Come to think of it, Matt said he was jealous, but not really anything else about his feelings.

It was pretty clear how he felt upstairs.

But he had said something about going back to the real world and we acted like we had before Matt knew the truth.

Friends.

Really good ones, but friends, nonetheless.

At one point, his knee was resting against mine and I almost reached over to thread our fingers together, but didn't want to do anything in front of his brother if he wasn't comfortable.

Pulling next to the garage, even though they always tell me I can pull in and use one of the empty spots, I park and look around. It seems as if I'm out before everyone, so I walk up to the main house.

I hear a familiar thud from behind the house and veer around to say hi to Bryant, who must be chopping wood out back. Sure enough, the second-oldest Landen brother is setting up a new log when I come around the corner. There's an impressive pile of already-split wood lying to the side, but he's not even breathing hard, yet.

"Rough morning?" I ask, making myself useful by picking up the pieces and stacking them.

"Couldn't sleep much," he says, his deep voice sounding worn. "Figured I'd get a jump start on this."

I look at the cords of wood, chopped and ready.

"Are you behind?" I ask, still getting used to what's normal around here, but honestly, it looks like they have enough wood for four different fires to burn nonstop for a full year without running out.

He snorts. "Never."

Chuck has definitely given Bryant a hard time about how often he needs to blow off steam by splitting wood.

"Want to talk about anything?" I offer. He's not known as being chatty, but sometimes he's more apt to have a conversation than others.

"Nah," he says, shaking his head and bringing his axe down, easily splitting the wood in half. "But I appreciate you asking."

"Anytime. Really."

He tips his head towards the house. "Coffee's ready if you want to head in."

"Want me to bring you a cup?"

"I'll be inside in a couple minutes."

I nod and grab a few more pieces of wood, putting them away and going around the house to the front door. I know I can use the back door, but I rarely see anyone other than Bryant using it and since his bedroom isn't far from that entrance, it feels more like his door.

The sound of the axe hitting the next log repeats until I'm inside and close the door behind me. I'm stepping out of my boots when Tommy comes down the stairs, yawning.

"Good morning," Tommy says. "Did you eat?"

"Nope," I say.

He smiles. "Good, I'm glad you're getting used to having breakfast with us."

I follow him to the kitchen where there's a quiet conversation happening. My heart rate picks up. Jax is probably at his place with Avery, so that leaves Chuck and Matt to most likely be talking.

"Look who's joining us," Tommy announces when we enter the space.

Chuck smacks me on the back. "We'll make a true cowboy out of you, yet."

Matt's mouth twitches like he's fighting back a smile, but he stays where he is, leaning against the counter next to the stove where it looks like over a dozen eggs are cooking. He has some major bed head on one side.

"Sleep well?" I ask, keeping my tone light around his brothers.

He smirks at me and it's so sexy. "Like a damn baby."

Chapter 35
Matt

"You do know that babies are notoriously terrible sleepers, right?" Chuck draws my attention as he gets the creamer from the fridge.

I'd much rather have my hands all over Caleb right now instead of rolling my eyes at my brother, but the eggs are almost done, so I'm not going to get what I want right now.

"Since when are you an expert on babies?"

"Uh, Christy?"

"Who's Christy?" Caleb asks.

"A single mom he was seeing a few years ago. But wasn't her kid four? That's not a baby." I remember just how cautious Chuck was to not do anything that could hurt or confuse the kid.

"That's not the point."

"It is when you claim it as proof of your expertise." Apparently having to make eggs so the right amount are over-easy while the rest are over-medium and not taking Caleb up to my room right now is making me cranky and slightly argumentative.

Tommy and Caleb fill a couple of mugs with coffee

"Someone woke up on the wrong side of the bed," Chuck grumbles, confirming my theory that I am, in fact, getting less pleasant to be around.

"All I said was that I slept well," I say, knowing this conversation doesn't need to continue, but I'm already knee deep in this argument.

"How does Bryant take his coffee?" Caleb asks, louder than necessary, but it's effective in getting Chuck and I to stop.

"Black," the three of us reply in unison.

He chuckles and takes the creamer from Chuck to put in two of the three mugs in front of him, handing one to me. It's just the right shade, which means he used the perfect amount of creamer.

"Thank you," I say, our fingers brushing as I take the mug from him, feeling warm inside.

Would it be appropriate to kiss him right here in the kitchen with Chuck and Tommy here?

"No problem," he says, like it's not a big deal we made contact or him knowing exactly how I take my coffee isn't something I'd notice. But before he turns around to bring his and Bryant's coffees out to the table, I catch a little blush appearing.

I go back to getting the rest of the eggs onto the platter and pull the sausage, bacon, and English muffins out of the oven.

The back door opens and Bryant steps out of his boots before coming over to wash up.

"Caleb got coffee for you already," I let him know.

I get a grunt in return. It's not a cranky grunt or a rude one. Just his way of acknowledging what someone says. But, for the second time this morning, I feel like pushing for something.

"Feeling better?" I ask.

"Who said I wasn't feeling good?"

I give him a deadpan look, sighing at my lack of patience this early in the morning.

He huffs out a breath. "I wasn't sleeping so I got ahead on prepping firewood."

"Ahead of us losing power for a few years and needing to run everything off of chopped wood?" The sarcasm in my voice isn't lost on him.

Another huff as he dries his hands and then he gives me a noogie like he did when I was little. "You're a smartass this morning, anyone tell you that?"

"Only the guy who thinks we could potentially run out of wood in the next decade."

He rolls his eyes at me, grabs the platter of protein, and brings it to the big table with me following. I set the carbs in the middle and take a seat next to Caleb with my coffee.

I'm not really sure what's going on with me this morning. I woke up in a pretty damn good mood and then Chuck went and interrupted my conversation with Caleb, getting right on my nerves. It only takes a minute, while food is being passed around the table, to figure things out.

Chuck interrupted my conversation with Caleb.

I told Bryant that Caleb basically went out of his way to get coffee for him the way he likes it and Bryant didn't really say anything.

Each time I got to talk to Caleb or touch him, I felt good. And each time someone doesn't see how amazing he is or interrupts us, I get petulant.

I put together my breakfast sandwich quickly, cutting it in half so it's easier to hold with one hand then casually drop my free hand into my lap. While Caleb is about to take his first bite and listening to Tommy explain something from one of the last meetings he was at with Samatha Jones, I slip my hand onto his thigh.

The response is instant. He doesn't look over at me, but he takes in a sharp breath and bites his bottom lip. Then he shifts so his knee is touching mine and I have better access to him without reaching too far and giving away that I'm rubbing his leg.

I feel in control of myself and my emotions again. Grounded even.

Turned on, too.

Doing anything under the table beyond this would be way too obvious because the chairs are a little spaced out, but it's enough. Maybe it's reminding me that yesterday happened. That the note I've read over a hundred times since he went home is real.

Either way, I'm really looking forward to getting away with Caleb for a few hours.

Maybe I'm really into thighs.

Or maybe I'm really into Caleb's thighs since I've spent the entire car ride so far with my hand on his right one.

Am I tempted to move my hand higher? Hell yeah.

But I'm trying my best to behave and let him concentrate on driving the hour each way on top of going to the rodeo and out to eat. It's a lot of concentration and there will be a lot of stimulation with the lights and sounds at the rodeo and I really want this to be good for him. So he can let go.

As usual, once we're on the highway and he's done shifting, half of his left arm is out the window. My window is down, which is fine, but I'd rather keep my limbs inside the vehicle. The wind is fairly loud in the truck so we don't do much talking, but that's alright. Things are calm and steady.

His phone rattles in the spot that was once an ashtray. Caleb keeps his eyes on the road though and asks if I'll check it.

"Something from Cooper," I report.

"Would you mind reading it in case something happened with the tickets?" he asks.

I'm really not sure how there would be an issue because Cooper had physical tickets delivered to the apartment last night and I know this because Caleb has pulled them out to make sure he has them about fifteen times today.

Typing in his code, I unlock the phone and read the message aloud. "Last chance for the campaign, I'm meeting with the rep in an hour."

He sighs dramatically.

"Would you like me to respond with anything?" I ask.

"Is there a polite way to remind him I passed on this three times already? And that they're all in our emails?"

Part of me is happy he's passing on this contract. It's the water one where he'd be in New York for a while. If he felt like he needed the work for any reason or if he had shown any interest in taking it, I'd support that fully. But I like that he seems to want to just stay put.

"What about saying that you're good and if he needs wording for turning down the offer that you can send him something?"

He pulls his left hand into the cab and onto the wheel while his right grabs my wrist and plunks my hand right back onto his thigh. Then he switches everything so his arm is out the window again.

"Yes please, but keep that right where it was," he says, looking down at the way my fingers are squeezing his leg.

Shortly after I send the message, we're pulling into the parking lot. Not surprising, it's pretty full, so we have a bit of a way to go, but I don't mind. It's a beautiful day so a little more sunshine won't hurt either of us.

"Are you ready?" I ask, rubbing my hands together excitedly as he comes around the bed of the truck so we can walk to the gates.

His smile is stunning and I can see those flecks of gold in his brown eyes.

"Hell yes," he replies as we walk side by side.

After a couple of steps, I feel a hand starting to slip into mine and suddenly everything happens involuntarily. My steps falter, my chest tightens, and, like they have a mind of their own, my hands bury themselves in my pockets before anything else can happen.

Just like that, in less than a day of kissing the man of my dreams, I know I've fucked things up, but I can't even begin to process how to fix it.

Chapter 36
Caleb

What the fuck?

"Is everything okay?" I ask, hoping that I misread him blatantly putting his hand in his pocket when I went to hold it.

"Yep." There's something in his tone that makes me want to haul him back to my truck and talk to him.

"We were just—"

"Just what?" he cuts in, a challenge in his eye.

I pause, reality hitting me like a fucking hoof to the chest.

Matt has only been affectionate with me in private so far. At best, I'm what, a fling? Someone to scratch an itch? At worst, he's been taking pity on the fallen rodeo star with no real family who imposed himself on the Landen brothers because the youngest one feels like home.

God none of that feels fair to even think, but what am I supposed to do when we haven't talked?

"Nothing," I say, a tight-lipped smile on my face in an attempt to hide the pain. "Just forget it."

Fumbling in my pocket, I grab the tickets, handing him one. "Why don't you go in? I forgot something in the truck and I'll meet you inside."

He frowns and looks down at me. "I'll walk back with you."

Jesus, Mary, and Joseph, I just need a fucking minute to think so I can get my head on right. I can feel tears pricking at the back of my eyes and look away, trying to blink them back.

"I don't want you to miss anything on my account. I've seen plenty over the years." My hand holds his ticket closer to him and he shoves his hands deeper into his pockets. God, he's as stubborn as me sometimes. "Just take the damn ticket, Matt."

His jaw clenches. "No."

And then he walks past me back to the truck.

"Seriously? I don't need a fucking babysitter," I grumble. That's the role he defaults to now, I suppose. That's what everything between us has been. Pity and taking care of his friend. His buddy.

The only sign he's bothered by my comment is the tensing of his shoulders. His stride stays sure and pissed off as he leads the way. I pinch the bridge of my nose and hold in a scream of frustration. What does he have to be so mad about?

Thankfully, since we were the last ones in this row, no one else is in view so I don't have to mask my emotions. I just need to keep everything at bay long enough to get into the truck. Surely he'll wait outside.

Oh fuck, he's going to expect me to actually grab something. I wrack my brain for a second until I remember that I have a pack of gum in the glove box. That's better than nothing.

The gravel crunching under our boots feels like it's amplified. Matt's head shakes every now and then, but he doesn't say a thing until we're at my truck.

He turns to face me by the taillight, his expression detached, hands still stuffed as far into his pockets as possible. "Well? Grab what you needed so badly."

His tone is clipped, setting me on edge.

"I didn't ask you to come with me. You could be watching the damn rodeo right now." I walk past him and go to the driver's side to buy myself a moment of privacy, trying my best to ignore the pull I feel towards him.

Just thirty seconds to get myself together.

I turn my key and unlock the door, pressing the button to open it with a satisfying pop. Hauling myself into the seat that gave me freedom, I will my emotions back. I can deal with them later. With the door closed I squeeze my eyes shut and try to take a deep breath.

A sharp knock on the passenger window startles me in my half-a-second to get my shit together. Matt's staring pointedly at the depressed lock and I groan in frustration as I lean over to unlock it.

The annoyance radiates off of Matt who still isn't looking at me as he plunks himself down and slams the door shut, closing us in a deafening silence. God, was it less than a minute ago that he kept his hand on my thigh and everything felt right?

"Well?" he says once more, this time gesturing around the cab with both hands.

Again, I ignore the pull as I reach over his lap and pop open the glove compartment. It falls open with a clunk above his knees. Grabbing the cotton candy flavored bubblegum, I do my best to touch his thigh as little as possible as I slam the glove compartment shut.

A derisive snort leaves Matt. "Really? This is what you needed so badly?"

My patience is about to snap.

"Yes," I bite out. Pocketing the gum, I reach for the handle only to feel Matt's arm across my chest, stopping me. He presses my lock down.

"Just," he starts, letting out a sharp breath, pulling his hand to his lap, and shaking his head. "Just…"

I wait in the charged silence, slowly counting in my head, giving him time to speak.

I get to sixty.

Nothing.

"Look," I say, with only a slight wobble in my voice, unlocking my door with a flick of my thumb and setting one of the tickets between us. "I misread things. I won't do that again. Please lock your door when you leave."

With that, I haul-ass out of my truck, hitting the lock as I swing the door shut. I'm almost jogging to stay ahead of my emotions. Each step feels like a coil is winding tighter inside of me, getting closer to snapping. Once I reach the gate, I hand over my single ticket to get scanned, unsure of what's being said in my hurry to get someplace alone. The moment it touches my fingers again, I make a beeline to the bathrooms on the second floor, away from the main concessions.

To my relief, it appears to be empty, and I'm at the last stall before I realize it, shutting myself inside and letting my head fall back against the locked door. A choked sob tries to escape me, but I smother it with my hand, biting my knuckles and letting out a groan of frustration to force everything down.

Feeling my teeth against my skin helps push the heartbreak down deep. Because in this moment, I can call it what it is. It's not disappointment. It's not confusion.

It's a clear rejection of me. And my heart can't handle it, not here.

I'm such a fucking idiot.

I likely just ruined any chance of putting down roots in Greenstone. Yeah, the brothers will still be great, but Matt fucking knows that I want more and he clearly doesn't. It's not like it's fair to either of us to be friends in public and fuck around when we're alone until he moves on.

No, I just need to get my shit together for the rest of tonight and be his buddy again. I'll buy my own god damn ranch if I have to so I'll have a reason to leave.

Just not tonight. Tonight I just need to be the friend he's had and nothing more.

With that, I shake myself to loosen up and gently slap my cheeks, pushing out a fast breath. I don't give myself time to close my eyes or think about what he was going to say in the truck or why he didn't let me go alone. My apartment is the place where I can pick through every damn detail until I've analyzed it twelve different ways.

Not here. Not now.

The sound of the lock sliding out of the latch feels loud in my ears and the door swings on squeaky hinges. Not hearing or seeing another person, it feels safe to go to the sink, the water refreshingly cold. Splashing some over my eyes to cool them from almost crying helps the redness I see in the mirror and I take a few breaths. I can't stop to let things build up again, otherwise, I'm going to fall apart. No, tonight is about entertainment and having fun with my...

My what? Best friend? Definitely not my boyfriend. Rolling my head back to release some tension in my shoulders, I take one more look in the mirror and leave every emotion in that last stall on the right, let numbness wash over me, and leave the privacy this space afforded me.

I stop in my tracks when my feet cross into the hallway because leaning against the wall, head down, hands back in his pockets, is Matthew Landen.

Chapter 37
Matt

It's like my voice is betraying me.

I can't speak the words.

No, I can't even think the words to try to speak them.

All I could do was lock his door and sit there, frozen. When he left his truck, it took about ten seconds before I realized what he said and that he was going inside.

He needs space.

Which is how I found myself trailing after him but not calling out his name.

As much as I want to follow him into the bathroom, I force myself to stay right here. And my traitorous hands are back in my pockets again.

I don't wait long before he comes out.

His eyes are a little red and he closes them when he sees me.

"Let's go watch. If you want to talk about anything later, that's fine, but let's not ruin today because I was an idiot." His voice is tight.

I want to ask him what he thinks he was an idiot about when I'm the one who fucked up. But I can't. I'm just standing here, only able to nod.

How do I explain to him what happened in a way that doesn't freak him out? He already knows I'm a little messed up and that much of it is rooted in feeling responsible for our mom leaving.

Oh God, he's already walking to the seating area. I'm still standing here, watching him.

Finally, my feet move and I'm jogging to catch up. Unfortunately, by the time we're side by side again, it's like my tongue is stuck in place.

So I'm just quiet.

While he thinks he did something wrong.

Fuck.

This is not how I wanted today to go. I didn't have specific expectations or anything, but this was the last thing from my mind.

Right before we reach the stairs, I put my arm out and stop him.

"Your earplugs." Now my mouth works.

"Good point," he says, pulling out his case. "Wouldn't want to need a nap before we drive home."

Even with the shitfest that just went down, hearing him refer to "home" as somewhere near me makes my heart skip a beat.

"How's this?" he asks, checking the volume of his voice, which is usually louder than needed right when he puts them in.

Like a complete dork, I give him a thumbs up and say, "Let's go."

When his back is facing me, I roll my eyes at the way I'm acting. We're about to watch the rodeo, something I've enjoyed my whole life.

It's time to breathe in the smell of the horses, bulls, leather, beer, and concessions. To let the roar of the crowd drown out all the ways I screwed up in the last ten minutes. To have fun with my best friend.

"The way they rode today, not one of those riders would have stood a chance against you even on your worst day," I say as we finally reach the truck.

It's the first time we've been able to say more than a handful of words to each other since we stepped into the stands. The crowd quickly recognized him, and he had a pretty constant line of fans hoping to talk to him or get his autograph.

He looked stunned at first and I put my hand on his back so he knew I was there for him. Then he relaxed and turned on the charm that has made half the country fall in love with him.

"Some of the guys seemed to have an off day, that's for sure," he says, taking out his earplugs and putting them away.

The engine roars to life and he pulls out of the parking lot with ease, thanks to all the people wanting to talk to him and slowing us down. It was all worth it, even if we're leaving later than we planned. He looks proud and confident.

"Would you be up for bar food?" I ask, trying to sound casual.

"Do you have someplace in mind?"

"If you're okay with it, I was thinking of checking out Shady Saddles over on Clairmont and Fifteenth."

"Sure," he says.

And I wait, thinking there's something else coming.

"Do you need directions?" I ask.

"Nope," he says, popping the *p*. "One of the perks of being here so much over the last decade is that I can find a few of the places without guidance."

I'm not sure if that's a dig at me for making him feel like he should need help, or if he's just confident. Usually his confidence comes off less self-deprecating, if that's what you can call his tone.

One knee bounces with nerves. I'm pretty damn confident that this is a good idea. Plus, I called the place last night after Caleb went home to make arrangements. Whatever he had in mind for dinner should, hopefully, pale in comparison.

Part of me wants to tell him why I want to go to a grungier bar, but that would ruin the surprise. He's been so content in Greenstone, but he's lost that swagger that came with being the best at what he does. Or having what he was the best at taken away so suddenly.

"It seems to be rodeo themed," he comments while pulling into the parking lot and rolling up his window.

"So it does," I reply, keeping my cool.

The lot is fairly empty because it's too early for the dinner rush, which is perfect.

"You shouldn't need those for a bit," I say as he's pulling out the container for his earplugs.

He raises an eyebrow in question, and I shrug.

"Just trust me."

It's a small shift, but he relaxes when I say it.

"Come on, cowboy, let's get dinner." This time, I remember to lock the door on my own.

When we're walking to the entrance together, I'm reminded of Caleb trying to hold my hand earlier. The panic is almost gone now and I even have the small urge to hold his, which is huge progress. But that would be a dick move. We need to be able to talk about it. If we can't and I freeze up again, I'm only going to be playing games with him.

I hold the door open for him so he can see what's just to the right of the bar. This time he stops in his tracks. He looks back at me, his brown eyes wide with surprise, and I just smile and say, "Well, what are you waiting for?"

Chapter 38
Caleb

There's a mechanical bull.

I feel like a kid in a candy store.

I look back at Matt whose smile is damn infectious.

"You planned this?" I ask, knowing the answer. He wouldn't have picked this place otherwise.

"They'll keep the music at a lower volume until six so you shouldn't have to wear your earplugs for a bit, and they promised to keep the bull at lower speeds when you're on so I don't have a heart attack worrying about you getting hurt."

The urge to kiss this man is terrible, but I will respect his boundaries. Instead, I give him a quick hug and mumble a sincere, "Thank you," next to his ear. God, I want to linger, but he's been my best friend for years and I can figure out how to get back to that because losing him would crush me.

Seriously, how many people have a friend who would set this up?

"Get up there," he says, gently pushing me towards the guy at the controls.

The name tag on this guy's shirt reads *Chris* and he tells me the safety rules as Matt double-checks that he'll keep things slower and steadier.

Honestly, I don't mind one bit that it won't be a live bull or that Chris can't open it up to full speed. Just being able to do this at all feels like I'm getting a little piece of my old self back.

I step up onto the huge mats surrounding the bull, noticing they have a lot of give and cushion to them, which should put Matt at ease. Then I put my hands on the machine, first noticing that it's not radiating heat, but that they used a faux fur on it, giving it more of a realistic feel against my palms. Pushing up and tossing my leg over is completely natural. Except I'm not caged in getting settled on a bull ready to do its damnedest to buck me the moment the gate opens and it has some room to move. The lack of saddle feels empowering even though this is a controlled environment and a mechanical bull.

The rope is nothing compared to what I'm used to, but sliding my fingers under it and gripping it tight with my knuckles facing up makes something click into place. My hips settle and my thighs squeeze tight in anticipation of the movement to come. When my hand goes up and I nod to signal I'm ready to start, there's a surprising jolt where the bull's backend dips down but my body automatically leans forward, keeping my balance easily. The motions smooth out but vary in angle and position.

Damn, this feels good.

I feel so comfortable that I almost let go of the rope and turn around on the bull so I'm backwards.

Almost.

Knowing that Matt would lose his mind with worry has me enjoying this ride exactly as intended.

When I look up after being spun around a few times, I expect to find him smiling. Or laughing at how easy this must look for me. But what I see over his phone, which is likely recording the event so I can watch it later, is something I assumed was off the table between us...

Hunger for me.

It's the look that was on his face right before he kissed me for the first time. The same look he had when he gave me that tiny peck on the lips and I complained that he shouldn't be allowed to only kiss me once and he came back and kissed me like it was his dying wish.

Honestly, if this bull was going at full speed right now, I'd likely fall off from the shock of how unguarded his expression is after whatever went down earlier today.

Luckily for me, moving with the bull on these settings doesn't take any thought and instinct takes over completely, keeping me steady. But damn it all to hell, if I don't hold eye contact as long as I can before the bull rotates so I can't see him easily.

It's a struggle to keep my mind open and free. I want to enjoy this to the fullest and not overanalyze whatever is, or is *not*, happening with Matt beyond our friendship and this ride.

My back muscles and abs are getting a workout, that's for sure, even with my regular exercises plus work at the ranch. Something about the motions makes muscles I normally don't notice burn since I haven't been training regularly.

And it makes me feel so alive to reclaim this. To let myself ride in a way that won't put me back in the hospital for another month or two.

Who knew a mechanical bull would mean this much after my accident?

I can feel the shift as the bull slows down before coming to a stop. I take an extra few seconds for a deep breath of appreciation before swinging my leg over and dismounting onto the blue mats. My thighs are going to be a little sore tomorrow and I can't wait to feel that burn again because it's different from a long day in the saddle.

Checking the name tag before I clasp his hand, I thank Chris for the ride and look at Matt. He's smiling now, looking happy for me, and maybe a little proud.

"You looked great up there," he says, sticking his hands in his pockets.

"I can't thank you enough for planning this. I didn't know how much I needed that," I admit.

He dips his head in acknowledgment. "It's been a tough few months and what you said yesterday got me thinking of things you *can* do, because we've had to focus on what you *shouldn't* for safety. This seemed like a good idea."

Since he has his hands in his pockets, I don't give him another quick hug. It seems the best thing to do is to shove my hands in my own pockets and keep them to myself. "Well, I really appreciate it, Matt. Really."

He clears his throat and looks around the bar. "Want to pick a table and order some food?"

"Let's do the corner by the windows," I say, then lead the way.

Matt sits across from me and, even though I wouldn't call the place *loud*, it's less noisy over here. It's darker than I expect, too, but it looks like the light above our table has a burnt out bulb.

"Do you want a different table in a brighter spot?" I ask.

He glances above the table and then at the ceiling around us.

"We can move if it's bothering you," he says, rubbing the back of his neck like he does when he's a little embarrassed or nervous. "I may have asked them if it was possible to have a dimmer environment for a few hours so you'd be less likely to overdo things before driving back. It looks like they just turned off half the lights to make it happen."

I can't really do anything but stare at him. Sure he's my emergency contact and is the person who knows me the best, especially with regard to my recovery, but I'm blown away by how thoughtful he's being. If we were together, I'd lean across this table and kiss him.

But I can't, so I stare.

Chapter 39
Matt

Fuck, I said too much.

Now it looks like I don't think he can handle being in a restaurant without needing a nap to recover or something.

Thankfully, a server comes over to our table with menus and takes our drink orders. Instead of getting a little liquid courage, I order a soda just in case Caleb doesn't want to drive the whole way back. Plus, I don't want him to feel odd for not drinking. It just isn't a good combo even if he only had half a beer with his recovery still in process.

Without the help of liquor, I gather my courage and keep my eyes on the menu, pretending to read it over when I say, "Hey, can we maybe talk tonight at your place?"

My voice is nice and casual, like this isn't me trying to schedule a time to talk about what a weirdo I am with holding hands. I don't want to wait to have the conversation, but I really don't want to have it here, and I don't want to make him feel trapped in the car while he's supposed to be concentrating on driving. Waiting until tomorrow would definitely be pushing the limits of my patience since I've had a few hours to find my words. Or at least some of my words.

"Of course," he replies, equally engrossed in his menu.

Part of me expects him to ask what I want to talk about, but I'm sure he's already guessed that the topic has to do with the two of us.

"Thanks."

"Want to try a bunch of things? This menu is massive and I'm feeling good," he says with a bit of a twinkle in his eyes.

"One dish from every section, maybe?" I challenge.

"I'll take vegan, soups, seafood, entrees, and cold apps while you grab the rest, but we both order a dessert? And we keep it a surprise."

"On it."

We both pull out our phones and start taking notes for what we're ordering. We're going to have so many leftovers. I finish making my selections a minute before Caleb and I take that time to simply enjoy being with him.

I really fucked up earlier today and I need a less-stressful place to get my words in order. The car ride will be perfect for that. So I cut myself some slack and watch him decide what to order. Some of his curls fell out of the front of his hat and rest on his forehead. He's sucking on his bottom lip in concentration, something I rarely see, but it makes me want to pull that lip into my mouth again.

After I apologize, of course. Maybe grovel.

Possibly on my knees.

Oh God, the idea of wrapping my lips around him has me getting hard instantly. Good thing we're sitting at a table in the darker corner of this bar.

I briefly wonder if I should have practiced on something by now. My gag reflex can't be that bad. I know it's important to relax and can figure out some of those little tongue tricks that feel amazing.

Caleb looks up with that thousand-watt smile of his and it falters when he makes eye contact. Shit, everything must be written clearly all over my face.

"All done?" I ask without even thinking about how my voice might be filled with need.

He swallows slowly, obviously reading me like a book. Then he blinks a few times, like he's clearing his mind.

"Yeah, I'm getting really excited."

Someone walks towards our table and we both shift to watch our server bringing our drinks.

"Here ya go," he says. "Are you ready to order?"

Caleb nods. "We're ordering to share but are keeping it a surprise until you bring it out, if that's okay with you."

"Sure." The server seems amused and leans over to read Caleb's screen and writes the order on his pad. "Got it."

He comes over to me and I hold my phone so he can read it. He writes for a minute then looks up at us.

"Appetizers first, then the main dishes, followed by desserts?" he asks.

"Yes, please," Caleb replies.

"Alright, I'll put this in and time it so you two can head out before six when it'll be brighter and louder again."

"Are you the manager I spoke to last night?" I ask.

"Yep, and it was a pleasure to see you ride Mr. Harlow."

"Thank you," we both say.

"Not a problem." With that, he walks back to the bar to enter the massive order.

"He's getting one hell of a tip."

"We're racking up one hell of a bill for two people," I say, laughing.

"True, but I get to pay," Caleb says.

"I picked the place," I argue.

He shakes his head. "I get to pay."

For some reason, this means a lot to him.

"Alright," I say, even though I wanted to pay for this since he got the tickets. I know he says he can retire, but some of those rehab bills are no joke even with his insurance.

"How did it feel watching today?" I ask, unsure if there's a better way to word that question.

He steeples his fingers under his chin and purses his lips while he thinks. Nothing in his body language makes me think he's annoyed that I asked, so that's good.

One less thing for me to apologize for later.

"It was a little weird," he begins. "I mean, I've sat out a couple of events due to injury, but I haven't spent the whole time in the stands in…I don't know how long. Being back with the sounds, sights, and smells was a little bittersweet since it's different now. When the riders were out, I found myself analyzing them in new ways."

"How?" I ask.

"It was like I was watching their form to predict how they'd do during their ride, whereas before, I was watching my competition. I'd still watch for things I could incorporate into my riding to get better, but this was different."

"You'd make a damn fine teacher if you ever wanted to train anyone." I mean it, too. There might be something that makes riding so natural to someone like Caleb, but you don't get to his level without putting in the work.

He shrugs. "I'd have to live somewhere with a full facility to do that."

"Not necessarily, you could still live in Greenstone."

Or at Landen Acres.

"Commuting sounds terrible," he grumbles.

"There are options if you want to train people. You have enough of a reputation where people would come to you. Or you could run clinics once or twice a year and only commute for those."

I'm not sure where all of these ideas are coming from other than wanting him to be happy and to stay if he can. That is, if there's something he wants to stay for.

Or someone.

Doubt creeps in right away. Because why wouldn't it? Especially after my glorious display of dickery a few hours ago. There're plenty of reasons for him to *not* stay.

"I could do that." His words pull me out of my mini-spiral and I almost thank him. But if I did that, I'd have to explain what those thoughts were and to do that, well, that's the conversation for tonight.

And for the first time, I want to tell someone who isn't Mary.

Chapter 40
Caleb

"I can settle where I want and stay connected to the circuit without it ruling my life." The more I think about it, the more I like it. Cooper could probably look into options while keeping things non-committal for me.

It's hard to plan ahead when what I want is right across from me and he's giving me whiplash today.

Things feel better now, though. We're able to keep conversations flowing and it's a lot more comfortable.

I'll still need to keep things together until after Matt leaves tonight, but if I keep pushing those emotions down for a few more hours, then I can have fun now and then fall apart tonight.

This right here, this friendship, means too much to me.

We taste our way through egg rolls and bruschetta for our appetizers. Apparently, I'm eating incorrectly because when I shove my second bite of eggroll into my mouth, Matt gently chides me.

"Savor, Cay."

With my mouth full I sarcastically say, "And not scarf?"

He runs his hand over his face, shaking his head but smirking. "I can't take you anywhere."

"You can take me everywhere," I reply, smiling with one cheek filled with eggroll.

"I could," he says softly, like he didn't even mean for it to come out.

Now I'm confused all over again. I swear there were times today when he was about to kiss me, like the way he's looking at me right now—so intensely with those icy blue eyes. And then there were other times, besides the disaster I caused which I can't think about without needing to excuse myself, where he kept his distance around the crowds and even in the kitchen this morning.

"What's your favorite for the apps?" he suddenly asks, breaking whatever was happening between us and poking at the food on his plate.

I want, so badly, to say something. If he hadn't asked to talk at my place, I probably would. But I assume the topic later will have to do with us.

"I still need to try the salsa in the green bowl."

We can get through this meal, have fun, talk about whatever he needs, and then I can process it all tonight.

Finally, I pull into my parking space at my building. Matt's usually not a huge talker on car rides, but this one was even quieter than usual.

Within a few minutes, I turned the radio on with the simple goal of distracting me from thinking about whatever happened before the rodeo began.

Now it's quiet all over again because I killed the engine and no one is talking. Not that I expected the conversation he wants to have starting here.

Before I can ask him what he'd like to do, he's reaching into the back seat to grab the bags of leftovers, reminding me that we can still be friends even after sharing something yesterday. With that thought, I leave the truck, Matt following just behind, and I hold the door open for him.

Neither of us says a thing in the hallway, either. The main sound is the rustling of the plastic bags holding the food.

We've always been pretty good at just hanging out and never needing to fill any silences with idle talk. But this feels charged.

I knew leaving that note would change what we have. I don't regret it though.

My keys jingle as I turn the deadbolt first and then unlock the knob. It's still not enough to distract me from the tension buzzing inside me, especially smelling his spicy cologne that I love so much.

When we're inside, I watch him as we remove our boots. He's not really looking at me and he's still quiet, taking the food into the kitchen and putting it all in the fridge like it's natural for him to do that in my apartment.

Yes, he stocked my kitchen when I moved in, but if I wasn't so damn anxious, I'd likely be thinking about how easy it could be with him.

He shuts the fridge door and stops, staring at what's hanging from the cupboard handle above the pantry.

"And what do we have here?" he asks, pulling at the aprons to read what's printed on all three.

He gets to the one that says *Yes, chef* and turns to give me a sexy look with one eyebrow raised. He seems surprised I'm in the entryway even though I'm putting my hat away.

"I ordered them a little while ago and they arrived last night. I was planning on bringing one with me to the ranch this morning but forgot."

Why am I so nervous about something he said I should have there?

"We can bring it tomorrow morning," he says. "I noticed there are three..."

"Uh, yeah," I say, feeling a little ridiculous after everything that happened today. "I got two for here so you could wear one."

He nods and looks at the aprons one more time while I stay right where I am. It's my damn apartment, but I feel so out of place right now.

"Would it be okay if we sat down?" he asks, gesturing to the sofa.

"Yeah."

I'm hyper-aware of each step I take to get there. He's closer to the sofa and sits in his usual spot, leaving my favorite place open.

It's too quiet in here, but I wait for him to begin, trying not to assume anything. Instead of fixating on the list of what he might say that I've come up with already, I focus on one of the distressed spots of my jeans. My fingers rub the loose thread until it's a little ball before he softly clears his throat.

"Earlier today, I—"

"It's really okay, Matt," I interrupt and then blow out the rest of the air in my lungs in frustration. "I'm sorry, that was really rude. Please, say what you were going to say."

I don't have to be an asshole just because he wants some boundaries and I'd rather have none between us.

"I wanted to talk about why what *I* did wasn't okay, actually," he says, nudging my foot to get my attention.

"What do you mean?" I'm genuinely confused.

"The short version is pretty simple: I don't hold anyone's hand." He pauses and lets me process that, which I appreciate because, well, he held my hand in the hospital.

Was that some fluke? I try to remember any of the dates he brought to the rodeo over the years, but I can't picture him holding hands with anyone.

"Is there a long version you'd like to share? Because I'm pretty sure you held mine, unless I was having some ridiculously vivid dreams in the hospital."

He nods and looks down at his lap for a moment.

"I was still pretty young when my mom left, so I don't have a ton of memories from when she was still at the ranch. What I do remember most, though, was a feeling I had with her."

He rubs his thighs, the sound of his hands rubbing against the fabric filling the silence as he blinks a few times before continuing.

"She always held our hands. Our dad did, too, I guess, but she did it a lot from what I remember, and that always made me feel safe and loved. Then she left." Another pause. "And it wasn't like she needed to move for a job or something. No, she *left*. All of us. I think she tried calling me the most, but that was her own guilt she was attempting to alleviate."

He removes his hat and runs his hand through his dark blond hair.

"Ever since then, whenever someone would hold my hand, I wouldn't trust them. It took me a long time to bring it up with Mary after my dad died because it felt so insignificant considering everything that was going on. But she helped me understand where my need to emotionally and physically withdraw comes from."

I've never wanted to hold someone and never let go so badly in all my life.

Chapter 41
Matt

I'm not sure if I'm scaring him off. He's listening intently, which I hope is a good sign.

"All of that is to say that I'm really shitty at holding hands. My first instinct is to pull away from the person. It didn't take me long to figure out if I put my arm over someone's shoulders whenever I thought they might want to hold hands, they'd see it as a sign of affection. So, I was able to avoid it pretty expertly without having to ever say anything."

"Until today," he whispers.

"Until today," I agree. "Today, I went into that self-preservation mode, and I couldn't process everything fast enough to be able to talk about it."

"And I left you alone in the truck," he says, clearly feeling upset.

"Oh God, if you're feeling guilty for not giving me time to talk to you about it before we entered the arena, you would have needed to sit there for a few hours, so please don't. My head was spiraling and somehow blank at the same time. The only thing I could do was sit there in frustration at how I was handling it while not being able to do anything about it."

He's still playing with a little thread on his jeans, but now he's only looking at me.

"Thank you for letting me know," he says. "I'm sure that wasn't easy to tell me."

Everything was said genuinely, but something feels off. Maybe he's processing it all. But when he doesn't say anything else and he looks back at the little ball of thread he's made, it seems like he's trying hard to not be sad.

Then I realize that not only have I not apologized, but I haven't explained what I want. I was so busy trying to find the right words to explain the hand holding, that I didn't plan out how to talk about the rest.

Well, the first part I can do.

"I'm sorry."

"Matt, you don't have to apologize, it's not like we—"

"Stop. Please, stop." Just because I haven't figured out what to say, doesn't mean I'm okay with him finishing that sentence if there's even a remote chance he's about to mention us not being together, or not having an understanding.

Except he looks sad *and* tired now.

"I want this to work," I say, speaking the full truth.

He searches my face, likely for clues of my sincerity. I don't blame him after the shit I pulled today even though I explained the root cause.

"You want what, exactly, to work?" he asks.

"You and me. Together."

"What does that mean to you?"

I open my mouth to reply and freeze because I've pictured what our lives could be, but I've never really had a healthy relationship.

"You should probably know that I've been pretty terrible at dating in the past because I never wanted to let someone in who would leave. I would date people new to town as a way to appear to be going out with someone, just like everyone else. But I was doing that because the first month was just getting to know the basics. By the time things would get even remotely serious, I was gone."

"What are you saying?" he asks.

"That I've never had a healthy relationship. I don't have experience, other than artfully avoiding things. I'm not saying this to make excuses for anything I've already done. What I'm trying to say is that I wanted to make sure you have the full picture before potentially making up your mind for what you'd like."

"Okay," he says. "So, I'll ask you again, what does it mean to you when you say you want to be together?"

How is he so calm through this?

I'm wiping the sweat off my palms onto my jeans already because I'm so nervous. I'm not sure I've ever been so open with someone. Even Mary had a hard time getting me to be direct.

"I want to stay with you tonight and figure that out."

Honestly, I'm scared shitless of all the ways I could screw things up. But if we can spend enough time together with things out in the open, I'm hoping that will help us find some answers.

"Because you want to be together."

"Please tell me I didn't just think that and I said it out loud because, yes, that's what I want."

He leans forward and I'm drawn to him automatically. "I was just making sure. You haven't actually said anything after reading my note."

"Really?" I frown, trying to remember our conversations since then without much luck.

How have I not said I want him?

"Really." The right side of his mouth twitches and he scoots to the middle of the sofa. "Do you think we'll need the whole night just to talk?"

"I was thinking I could be a little creative with how I can further apologize to you." My hand rubs his thigh, staying close to his knee so we can talk more if he'd like.

Instead of saying anything else, he leans forward and presses his soft lips against mine. The tension I've been carrying around half the damn day starts to disintegrate with that simple contact. He pulls back only enough to break off the kiss and his lips brush mine again as he whispers, "Stay the night, please."

With that, the rest of that tension leaves me and I'm feeling secure enough that I didn't do irreversible damage to what I've been dreaming of having with this man. I toss my Stetson on the coffee table, then grab the back of Caleb's neck, drinking in this moment and not wanting to take any of this for granted.

My mouth coaxes his open and feeling his tongue sliding against mine is almost perfect except he's sitting too far away. I slide my hand up over his thigh until I'm gripping his hip and tugging him onto my lap. He tosses one leg over my lap so he's straddling me, and I pull him down so we're making as much contact as possible.

His fingers start undoing the buttons on my shirt, getting it off me in record time, and somehow I find the patience to do the same for the first few of his. Then I let out a frustrated sound and hope I've undone enough to get the shirt over his head without popping off the remaining buttons. His hands leave my chest while I lift the bottom of the shirt, realizing too late that I should have undone one more. Just when I'm lowering it so I can loosen more to give him a little more space to wiggle out, he moves his arms, which are over his head, and pops one, if not two, buttons and yanks the fabric off completely.

God, he looks like he was chiseled by an artist. His skin has that sun-kissed glow to it and my eyes trail down from his chest to find one defined muscle after another. As I look back up at his face, I catch a glimpse of the mark I left on his neck yesterday.

There's no reason to rush tonight.

This time, I'm going to savor everything.

Chapter 42
Caleb

"Hold on," Matt says and that's all the warning I get before he's standing up with his hands under my ass. There's a few inches of difference in our height, sure, and I know he's strong, but he's only straining a little, for crying out loud.

I let out a string of curses before my ankles are crossed behind him and my arms are looped around his neck. My momentary flailing doesn't slow him down though because we're already crossing the threshold to my bedroom. I'm not sure if anyone has ever picked me up like this. He's a man on a mission and I don't mind one bit.

"Shower?" I ask, thinking of the last time we were together.

"Not right now, cowboy," he says, striding to my bed. "We're simply not messing around on your couch like a couple of teens."

Somehow, his voice is even and only a little strained from carrying me. I know this man spends part of everyday doing manual labor, but even then, I'm no lightweight. The fact that he could just toss me on the bed with ease has me more excited than I would have ever thought.

Instead of throwing me down, he shifts one hand to the back of my head and lays me back, following along.

Right, because he doesn't want to give me a concussion.

It's actually really sweet to see him be so thoughtful when his eyes are burning with need and his bulge is pressing against my own. He's careful with our placement on my bed and I watch him look around to see the space between my hair and the headboard. I must be too close for his liking because he tugs us down a couple of inches before finally looking right at me once more.

"You'll tell me if I do something you don't like or you're not comfortable with, right?" he asks.

I rest my hand on the side of his face, my thumb rubbing across his cheekbone. "Like you're going to do anything I'm not going to like, Matt."

He blushes a little and rolls his eyes and I wonder what's making him nervous. Then I remember he mentioned not having dated guys before. That doesn't mean the same thing as never being with one, but it could, which would explain his possible lack of confidence. I pull him down so his lips are close enough to kiss.

"I promise I'll tell you."

Relief relaxes his features just enough that I think I've read him correctly. He may have plenty of experiences under his belt, but just like with everything else he does, he wants to get things right.

"Thank you, I'll do the same."

Then he kisses me, his lips so strong and sure. I practically melt into the bed as he takes the lead, his lips trailing down my neck with his tongue darting out right after he nips me with his teeth every now and then. When he gets to my bigger scar, he slowly, reverently, covers it in tender kisses. The scar itself has such little feeling, but the care he gives it makes my heart squeeze.

It's like he's making sure to lay claim to every part of me, even the parts where I see failure. But it gives me butterflies to watch the man who can tame a horse, throw hay bales around like they're toys, and more, be so gentle and sweet.

Next, he kisses his way to my tattoo, letting the tip of his tongue trace the outline of the stallion I have inked on my skin. My hips buck at the attention and he shifts his body down mine, taking my nipple between his teeth and giving it a gentle tug. All I can do is hold onto his shoulders and dig my nails in to anchor myself to him as he explores.

The sound that escapes me starts as a surprised grunt but turns into a moan when he chuckles with his lips on my nipple, flicking it with his tongue.

Watching me, he slowly and deliberately kisses down the center of my abs, moving lower and lower. His gaze is filled with desire and he doesn't look away until his lips are just above my jeans. This time, he pops my belt buckle open with surprising ease. I raise one eyebrow at him.

"I might have practiced while I cleaned it," he says with a smirk.

Normally, I'd give him shit for that, but I'm panting and entranced by both the sight and the feel of his fingers at the button of my jeans as he undoes everything. My underwear fully tents as my dick pops up and Matt opens his mouth and runs his teeth ever so carefully along my shaft over the thin fabric. I can't help but curse at how fucking amazing that feels.

"Up," he says, tapping the side of my ass, and I comply happily.

Pulling my pants down part-way while kneeling, he comes back for my boxer briefs, stretching them over my hard-on, his gaze catching on it for a moment before returning to his task. Pretty soon even my socks are somewhere on the floor and his hands run up my bare legs, squeezing my thighs as he goes.

"Finally," he whispers, then he dips his head and takes one long, slow lick starting at the base of my dick and moving all the way to the tip, letting out a long groan.

"Fuck," I bark out, surprised at how quickly he dove in.

Fisting my shaft just above my balls to keep it from twitching, he proceeds to lick me with the flat of his tongue like a damn lollipop until my dick is covered and slick from his saliva.

Maybe he's not as nervous about being with a guy as I thought.

Or maybe he's been with a guy and they just didn't date.

"You're fucking amazing," he says, and before I can respond to tell him how he's the amazing one, his tongue darts out over my tip, tasting my precum.

His eyes close as he swallows, his throat bobbing as he hums in approval. It's easily one of the sexiest things I've seen him do.

Which is saying something.

Chapter 43
Matt

Oh my God.

I was worried for a second that I might not like the taste, but that precursor just wiped that right out of my mind.

He's salty and just a little sweet, almost like salted caramel.

I open my eyes to see him watching me. His mouth opens as his chest rises and falls. His breathing is the only sound in the apartment right now.

"You taste like a damn dessert that I get to savor, you know that?"

Whatever his response might have been is swallowed up by the long moan he lets out as I slowly take him into my mouth for the first time.

Relax.

If I tense up, I'll gag for sure and I need to make sure my jaw is loose so my teeth don't hit his skin. It was sexy as fuck to watch his surprise and pleasure as I ran my teeth over his underwear though.

My lips are pushed farther apart as I reach the crown. I stay here for a few heartbeats, tonguing from his slit to the prominent ridge on the underside of his head. Bobbing down, I feel the silkiness of the skin covering his shaft while laying my tongue flat and shifting it from side to side.

Fingers grip my hair and I hum in approval, causing him to tug. That pull paired with the sounds he's trying to stifle go right to my groin.

Slowly, I work my way back up until I'm practically kissing his tip before quickly sucking in his head and pulling off once more. By the looks of things so far, the way I've gone about giving him a blow job has been satisfactory, which calms the voice of doubt that was trying to throw me off a few minutes ago.

When I go down this time, I take a little more into my mouth, keeping him from hitting the back of my throat. Once I have a rhythm that I hope won't have him finishing immediately, I start to explore more with my free hand as the other holds him steady while pumping, using the extra saliva I leave so everything is nice and slick.

Lord knows a chaffed dick is the worst.

His balls are a little hairier than mine and the coarse hair is darker, too. I cup and carefully roll them with my fingers, thinking of what feels good on me. He might have been right when he said he would like anything I do.

My heart pounds as I flatten out my fingers and press on his taint and move closer to his asshole without reaching it. He seems to like this even more than just gently playing with his balls. I know it's a spot when I'm with someone that gets ignored, but I always think it adds something.

But now I'm not sure what to do. Do I stay in this zone and keep working him? Do I explore more and test to see if he'd like some ass play?

Beyond looking it up online, I don't have experience in that. Not even on myself. I know he's been with other guys, but I don't know if he's a top, bottom, or vers, though.

Oh for fuck's sake, I need to go with the flow and get out of my damn head.

Thankfully, everything has been more than enjoyable on my end, especially all the ways he squirms in an attempt to not thrust.

He's panting now and I want to make sure he lasts a little longer, so this time, as I take him into my mouth, I pause, flicking my tongue in different ways. I press down farther than I have so far and my throat tenses.

Reminding myself to relax, again, I take a little more of him into my mouth and make it until he hits something, triggering a mild gag reflex that I hope is hidden by the sounds we're both making as we enjoy what's happening.

"Matt," he says, "I'm so close."

I raise my eyebrows at him in a silent question.

"Slow down, I want to touch you before I come," he says breathlessly, sitting up and squeezing his fists tighter in my hair as I give one final gratuitous lick. He flops down onto his back and gives me a devastatingly sexy smile. "Get out of those pants and get up here."

"Someone's getting bossy," I say with a chuckle, but already shucking my remaining clothes.

"Well, I've been drooling over the idea of having you in my mouth for quite some time and my patience is running low."

He looks so sure of himself lying there with one hand tucked behind his head, washboard abs, and massive erection. And all of that is mine to have.

At least for now.

I let out a little growl that's part-frustration at the voice of doubt in my head and part-desire because the man I've wanted for years just said *that* to me and I'm dying to try everything with him. While I crawl over him, he scoots himself to a seated position, resting his back against the headboard, taking my face in his hands, and guiding my mouth to his.

He takes the lead with a kiss that's unbridled with his tongue fighting with mine for the upper hand in a way I've never felt before. It's turning me on even more to have this side come out even though I'm usually the one in charge. The confidence pouring from him is the same as when he commands the attention of an arena full of spectators, winning their hearts with a smile and a wave.

His teeth tug at my lower lip and he fists my hair, pulling my head back so he can nip, lick, and kiss his way down my neck, and I grab the headboard so I don't fall completely on top of him. The combination of the surprise for each small bite with the soothing of his tongue and the scratch of his five o'clock shadow is driving me crazy with need. I can't decide if I like the feel of him better with or without his beard, but right now, I know anything on him would turn me on. By the time he's exploring my nipple, I'm the one panting and wanting to give myself one long stroke to take the edge off. His fingers mirror the motions on the other side while his other hand is pressing against my back and holding me in place. He watches me closely as he uses his tongue on my nipple, slowly adding his teeth while exploring my responses. When he's a little rougher and I gasp from the pleasure, he gives me a shit-eating grin.

"Good to know," he says, repeating the motion once more only to elicit a moan from me this time.

Chapter 44
Caleb

Feeling pretty satisfied with my discoveries so far, I think I've gotten Matt plenty ready. Not that he hasn't had one hell of an impressive boner this whole time, but he's leaking precum and it's too damn tempting to leave any longer.

I kiss my way down his abs. He's got a little padding over them so there's a little cushioning that I can press my lips into. I imagine that my lips leave an imprint after I move on. Dropping my hands to his hips, I guide him to a kneeling position and adjust how I'm sitting so my mouth is level with his dick.

"I need to tell you something," I say, my voice dripping with need as I gaze up at him, shifting one of his legs so his foot is on the bed and his knee is level with my shoulder. "I can't deep throat, but I don't have a big gag reflex for hitting the back of my throat."

It only takes a moment before his eyes widen in understanding.

"So, when I tell you that I want you to fuck my mouth," I continue as the headboard groans, presumably from his grip tightening, "I want you to be in complete control and take everything you want."

He stares at me, eyes ablaze and breath shuddering.

"If something is too much, I'll pinch your leg, okay?"

"Okay," he rasps.

I wish I could record the way he's looking at me. It's like I've unlocked something that he's tentatively letting out. Like the trust I'm giving him is precious.

My hands grab his ass and pull him close enough so my tongue can dart out and lick the liquid beads off. I enjoy the salty, musky taste of him for a moment.

"You taste like the perfect appetizer," I whisper, "and I can't wait to savor it."

I bring him into my mouth slowly, relaxing my jaw so he can fit as he lets out a long groan. Taking my time, I explore his head, flicking my tongue over the ridge and causing him to curse. Once I've got him worked up even more I press my hands against his ass again, feeding the first part of his shaft into my mouth.

"You feel so fucking good," he says, running one hand through my hair.

Before he can put his hand back on the headboard, though, I hollow out my cheeks and watch his mouth fall open as his fingers grip my hair tightly.

My God, he's the most beautiful person I've ever seen.

I pull off of him with a popping sound.

"Matt, I want you to fuck my mouth now," I say, knowing that he's plenty lubed up from everything I've been doing to him.

"You're sure?" he asks, his eyes hooded and his fist still gripping my hair tight.

"I'm sure," I reply, wrapping my lips around him and putting pressure on his ass once more.

He hesitates for a second before gently rocking his hips forward and pulling back, testing the waters. Tentatively, he starts to slowly thrust, keeping the motions fairly shallow. The whole time his gaze jumps from meeting mine to watching himself disappear into my mouth over and over.

After a bit, he finds a faster pace, occasionally pushing more of himself in while still being cautious. I move one hand to his balls, giving them attention and helping him relax more. That seems to encourage him to thrust harder, eventually hitting the back of my throat. I make sure I keep everything relaxed as he makes contact again and again.

I know I'm leaking once more because this is turning me on almost as much as his mouth on me. But I keep my focus on him, remembering when he added pressure to the place just behind my balls and shifting my hand to do the same.

"Oh fuck," he says, slamming the hand that had been holding the headboard against the wall.

If I could smile with his dick in my mouth, I would. Instead, I let out a hum of approval.

His thrusts come harder and faster as I watch a bead of sweat trickle down his chest.

"Where do you want me to—"

I cut him off by pressing the hand still against his ass harder so he knows not to pull out.

"Oh God, Cay," he moans, shuttling himself even faster until he's holding himself deep in my mouth, his legs shaking.

He grunts just before his cum hits the back of my throat and I greedily swallow each spurt down. I keep him in place, fisting the base of his dick, so I can lick him clean before letting him go.

He collapses on me and devours me in a kiss, loosening his grip on my curls and running his fingers through my hair. His other hand cradles the side of my face, his thumb brushing gently against my stubble. He rests his forehead on mine, catching his breath.

"Can I please make you come now?" he asks, his voice thick with desire.

"Fuck yes," I reply, grabbing a quick kiss before he's moving down the bed.

Without preamble, his mouth covers my dick and my hand grabs his shoulder automatically. I see red marks from when I gripped him earlier and think about the hickey still on my neck for anyone to see, making me harder as his tongue expertly works me.

A tingle starts deep inside me.

"Not long," I gasp out in warning.

Instead of pulling off, he adds his fist, working me into a damn frenzy. My balls draw up tight and I let out a whimper just before I'm seeing stars as I come. Waves of pleasure wash over me with the final pass his mouth takes. His tongue gives my tip one final swipe and I let out a shuddering breath, overstimulated after just coming.

He looks right at me, holding my full attention, and then swallows.

Swallowing or spitting or coming somewhere else has never affected me, but holy shit, that hit differently.

"You are so fucking amazing," I tell him, crawling the short distance between us to kiss him.

Unfortunately, he shifts his position as I reach him and I end up tackling him onto his back.

He bursts out laughing, which I'm not as worried about as when we were in the shower, and tucks me into his shoulder.

"You can just ask me to cuddle, you know," he ribs.

"Shut up and kiss me," I say with a smile, tilting his face in my direction with my hand.

"I think I can manage that, cowboy," he says just before his lips find mine.

Chapter 45
Matt

I'm happy.

For once, I refuse to allow all of my regular, intrusive thoughts to contradict what I feel with every fiber of my being. I'm even cuddling for fuck's sake. I'm usually pretty quick to find an excuse to shower or leave someone's place so I can retreat to the safety of my room.

"Before we go to sleep, remind me to message my brothers," I say.

"I can get off of you so you can get your phone," Cay says, starting to roll away from me.

"Nope. We're staying right here for a while."

He chuckles as I pull him tighter against me and he goes back to tracing patterns on my chest. We're still naked, but neither of us have moved, even when we stopped our mini make out session after he took me down like he was a linebacker.

"What do you need to message them about?" he asks.

"That I'm not coming home tonight," I say. That stupid doubt tries to creep in again though and I tense a little. "Unless you'd like to sleep alone."

He shifts so he's propped up on one elbow, looking down at me. "Why would I like to do that?"

I relax some. "Are you sure?"

"Matt," he says. "I want you to stay tonight and I want you to be in my bed with me."

He states it all so simply and so sure. It's hard for that doubt to argue against, which makes me smile.

"Alright."

"Good," he says, nodding and lying down on his side once more with his head resting on my shoulder.

We tangle our legs together and I lightly run my fingers over his bicep while he goes back to his patterns on my chest.

"What does this look like around other people?" His voice is even and non-judgmental. When I don't reply right away, he tries again. "I realize that yesterday was unplanned, but we kept our distance whenever we were around your brothers and in public. Knowing what boundaries you need would help me a lot."

"The hand thing is something I need to work on," I begin, knowing that it's important to avoid a repeat of what happened before the rodeo.

"What can I do to help you?" he asks, pressing a kiss to my chest. "I don't want to trigger you."

He waits patiently for me to gather my thoughts.

"If I can lead that for a bit, I think that would be best, so I'm fully ready for it and don't have a shitty reaction like earlier."

"Okay, that's doable."

"But I'd like to get to a point where I'm comfortable with it happening whenever and wherever." I look down at him and hope he can see how earnest I am. "Just because I haven't had a healthy relationship, doesn't mean that's not what I want. I don't want to fuck things up but might need help easing into it, if that makes sense."

"Would it help if we kept this," he says, flattening his hand on my chest for emphasis, "quieter for now while we figure out how to handle PDA-like things?"

Of course I want to say "no" right away, but I make sure to really weigh his words. Would it take some of the pressure off to be a "good boyfriend"? Absolutely. But do I want to feel like we're hiding anything? Not really.

"Do you mean just being friends? I don't want to do that."

"I mean taking the pressure off of figuring out what being a public couple means but still seeing each other privately and not anyone else."

"I don't like the idea of seeing you less," I admit.

"I'm not suggesting that. Good Lord, everyone would be asking questions if we suddenly weren't hanging out every day. What I mean is to give us a little time and privacy to practice how we'd like to be together in public. But it's only if you'd like that. You already know what I'm comfortable with," he says in a teasing manner and nips at my jaw. "I can keep my hands off you around other people if I get some regular alone time with you."

"And then what?" I ask, letting this all sink in.

"When you're comfortable with how you'd like to be together in public, you let me know." He shrugs and says it so matter-of-factly that it sounds easy.

"You'll let me practice holding your hand?" I ask.

"Any time you'd like."

"And we still get to see each other, but we take the pressure off of the public piece that I'm shitty at."

"Yeah."

"What if it takes too long?" I ask softly.

"We'll keep talking about it. When you want to practice and try things, we do that. When it's overwhelming, we pause. There's no timeline. I'm not going anywhere."

That's a lot to promise after less than two days together.

But I'm not one to judge because I'm not going anywhere, either.

"I don't want to mess this up."

"I know," he says. "I don't either."

"It's not hiding? I don't want it to feel like we're hiding."

"We're figuring things out together. That's all."

Something loosens in my chest. The pressure to go from a shitty boyfriend to one Caleb can be proud to have in public seems to have been heavier than I realized.

"Can I put my hand over yours right now?" I ask, feeling a little silly and a little brave.

"Of course," he replies. "You have my permission to do whatever feels right at any time."

I nod and try to not overthink what I'm doing. The thing is that I want to hold his hand. In the hospital, it felt right and I don't think it was just the extreme nature of the situation or the fact that he looked so alone. This is something that I can take back from years of doubts ringing in my head.

And I have one hell of a patient man helping me take baby steps to overcome it.

So I raise my hand off the bed as he keeps his nice and still on my chest. I think about all the encouragement Mary gave me for how I'll be able to be open with the right person. I just didn't expect I'd ever have a chance with Caleb, but it seems that I stumbled into possibly making my fantasies a reality.

My fingers brush over his hand and I relax my arm so my hand covers his. Our fingers aren't interlocked, and I don't feel like I'm trapped like this. It's an intimacy I can enjoy.

"I can hear your heart beating," he whispers, nuzzling his face against my chest.

I let out a soft laugh because it's definitely racing so I'm not surprised. "I can believe it."

We lie here for a few minutes, just like this. Neither needing to speak. Neither wanting to move.

That is, until I remember something.

"So, do I get the 'Whisk me away,' 'Yes, chef,' or 'Cooking up something good' apron when I'm here?"

"I believe it's 'Cooking up something *tasty*,' actually," he corrects with a huge smile. "I was going to bring the 'Yes, chef' one to the ranch and thought I'd let you pick what you'd like to wear here."

"I get to pick?" I ask. "It looks like I have a generous boyfriend."

"Damn right you do."

It's not until well after we've gotten ready for bed that I realize I called him my boyfriend out loud and that he agreed.

Chapter 46
Caleb

One week later

Is it getting harder to keep my hands off of this man when we're not alone?

Definitely.

Is all of this worth it to make sure we don't lose what we already have while working through things that need time to be addressed?

Also, definitely.

Is it kind of fun sneaking off and fooling around up in the loft?

Hell yeah.

But all those feelings aside, today is a huge day for Matt and he wants me here with him, so I've been on my best behavior all morning. Not once did I brush behind him too close, pretending to have lost my footing, in the stables while he was talking to someone. Not once did I so much as wink at him from across the corral while he rode the mare for the first time this very morning.

If I thought it would have made him feel better or taken his mind off his stress about lunch, I would have in a heartbeat. Hell, I would have tied a rope around his waist and hoisted him into the loft if I thought being on my knees would help him relax. But that's not what he needs today. He's a little fidgety, but his confidence is still high and he's damn determined.

I'm really proud of him.

We've talked about this so much recently so he has words ready to say. He even requested that I ask him the worst and most obnoxious questions I could think of so he could go into this prepared for anything. I don't think he needs to worry about his brothers not being supportive, but I understand where he's coming from.

"How are the carrots coming along?" he asks over his shoulder.

"You tell me," I say as I finish fanning the evenly sliced carrot sticks around the edge of the veggie platter.

"They look great," he says. "If I didn't know any better, I might think you've been practicing, but you must be a quick study."

"And when would I have time to practice without you knowing?" We haven't spent every night together since he called me his boyfriend because we don't want to call attention to anything, but we're still around each other all day.

"My point exactly. You'd be exhausted if you were practicing when we weren't together."

"Who's practicing something?" Chuck asks, waltzing into the kitchen.

"We were just admiring my chopping skills," I say while the tips of Matt's ears turn a little pink.

"They look good enough to eat," he says, tossing his toothpick into the garbage.

Matt gives him a deadpanned look. "That's literally what they're for...eating."

"It was a compliment, little brother," he replies, tousling Matt's hair.

"Too many people in the kitchen," my boyfriend says, pointing his spatula towards the dining room.

Chuck looks at my apron, smirks, then salutes Matt saying, "Yes, chef," before leaving.

Matt lets out an exasperated sigh. "He's going to be trouble, isn't he?"

I look out towards the dining room before taking a couple of steps towards him but stop before we're too close. "They're all going to approve. Chuck might be obnoxious at times, but you know he always wants everyone to be happy."

He nods and turns back to the stove, pulling the turkey burgers off and putting them on buttered and toasted buns.

"Should I bring out the tray?" I offer.

"Yeah, I'll follow with this and we can come back for the rest."

Normally, I eat decently, but since the accident, with Matt's influence, I've been eating better, especially in the vegetable department. If it wasn't for Matt, there's a chance this whole family would go a month without a green vegetable.

Jackson is filling his glass with water when I emerge from the kitchen and he fills mine before passing the pitcher to Tommy. After I set down the tray, Chuck comments on how the veggies are expertly chopped and I shake my head and chuckle. Is he being over the top? Of course. But that's one of the ways he connects with people. He gives them a hard time and makes everyone laugh.

I go back to the kitchen, passing Matt and making sure I don't turn around to watch the way his jeans hug his ass so perfectly.

I don't even have to look back at the table to know that Bryant is about to receive the pitcher. He's sitting opposite Jax as usual and by the time I come back with some of the other sides, he'll have filled Matt's glass. It's such a small thing, but everyone looks out for each other here.

And, somehow, I've been lucky enough to be brought into the fold, even without these guys knowing Matt and I are together.

It's not something I'm used to, that's for sure. Sure, my family ate meals together, but they were usually scattered and you took care of yourself. No one asked how you wanted your coffee. No one checked to make sure everyone had what they needed. It wasn't neglectful, but it wasn't the same as actively taking care of each other.

When I've gotten my apron untied and pulled over my head, Matt comes back to the kitchen, removing his. The hooks for the aprons are in the pantry and I take advantage of these few seconds where we're tucked away from everyone else.

Tugging on his belt and pulling him against me, I give him two quick kisses. "Are you ready?"

He looks collected and calm when he simply replies, "I am."

"Alright, let's bring the rest of the food out."

He catches my chin in his hand and holds me for two more kisses, these a little longer than those I gave him, but still faster than either of us would like.

We bring out the other sides, burger fixings, and saucers, and then take our seats. The guys reach to the center of the table for different platters and begin passing them around. Everyone gives Matt and me some sort of compliment on part of the meal over the next couple of minutes, but the conversation is minimal while we eat our first helpings until Jax goes around the table for updates.

Once we've covered upkeep, items to order or pick up, and the animals, Matt clears his throat. I drop my hand to my lap before shifting so it can rest on his thigh, offering silent support.

"I have something I wanted to bring up today."

Both Jax and Bryant raise their eyebrows while Tommy and Chuck set their next bites back onto their plate. These reactions are big enough for me to know that this is new territory for Matt. He contributes to conversations and decisions about the ranch, but I haven't seen him take the lead like this before.

Everyone is quiet and watches as Matt takes a deep breath before looking at each brother in turn.

"I'm building a house."

Chapter 47
Matt

Oh shit, that's not how I was supposed to start this.

"What I meant to say is that I'd like to do that," I say, backpedaling.

Caleb's hand gives my leg a comforting squeeze under the table.

Everyone is quiet, which only makes me want to squirm because they were all staring at me but now I'm looking down at the way my lettuce sticks out of my bun and start picking at it.

Another gentle squeeze from Caleb reminds me of all that we rehearsed.

My brothers being silent might have been the one thing we didn't think of. After a few more thundering heartbeats, Bryant's voice cuts through the silence.

"Where?" he asks.

I relax a little because I could have guessed his question would only be one word.

"The little rise across the stream about a mile from here," I say, hoping it makes sense to them.

"Oh," Tommy says, letting out a breath. "You mean you want to build a place here."

"Yeah," I say with a frown. "Didn't I say that?"

There seems to be a collective sigh of relief from all four of my brothers.

"You missed that tiny, yet significant, detail," Chuck says, ripping a piece off his bun and throwing it at me.

Jax throws his napkin at Chuck to get him to stop throwing things at me, which somehow works because it just makes Chuck laugh. The paper napkin only makes it a quarter of the way because it unfurls and floats down to the table harmlessly.

"So, you're not moving away." Jax's inflection is a mix between a statement and a question.

I shake my head. "No, I want—"

Oh God, I'm suddenly taken back to when they asked me what I wanted after Dad died. The pressure of waiting and needing someone *to say they truly wanted me to stay.*

And now I'm the one not talking. My tongue feels thick in my mouth, which is suddenly so dry. I grab my glass and down half of its contents.

"Matt," Bryant asks carefully, "is everything alright?"

Damn it, my chest is tightening and even though I know this isn't the same, my thoughts are starting to spiral just like back then.

The soft caress of Caleb's thumb tracing circles on my thigh reminds me that he's here with me, supporting me in whatever way I need. I look over at him and see nothing but patience, understanding, and support.

"Can you?" I whisper, motioning to myself.

"I'm here for whatever you need," he replies quietly.

I nod. My brothers have seen me shut down before, but they've never known why, not the full reason.

He clears his throat.

"Matt and I actually practiced this conversation the past few evenings because he's been nervous about a few things." My brothers' attention bounces between Caleb and me. "He wasn't sure if you'd all be up for another house on the property and knows that's a big ask. But..."

He looks me in the eye now with encouragement in his gaze. My chest loosens a fraction. Just enough to take in a gulp of air and finally speak the words that have plagued me for five years.

"The main reason was because I didn't want you all to think I'm ungrateful for everything you've done and that I wanted to leave. I don't know if I've been a burden since Dad passed or if you've wanted me to stay all along." I keep watching Caleb as I hear movement from my brothers, but they don't say anything. "None of you asked to be my guardian and, as much as I wanted to stay, I've always wondered if it would have been easier on you all if I had gone to live with Mom."

There's the truth of it all.

There's a clatter to my left, like Jax dropped his fork, and a loud, shocked, "What?" from Chuck.

"You thought we didn't want you here with us?" The pain in Bryant's voice is enough to pull me away from the safety of Caleb's eyes.

"I was a minor whose own mother was reluctant to take him."

"That one was on me," Jax admits. "I may have laid into her a little the day after he passed about her not taking you away from your home."

"You really thought you were a burden?" Tommy asks.

I shrug, incredibly uncomfortable at all this attention, while feeling a little lighter with each thing they say. "You all had to step in and raise me in your twenties. Except you because you were still a teen yourself. I didn't know what to think because no one told me anything."

Surprisingly, there's no resentment in my voice. I always assumed I'd be mad during this conversation and that it would be so much worse than this. But it's freeing to finally speak these truths that have buried themselves deep inside of me.

"For the past five years, you've thought this," Jax says. "So you had no idea what happened to make sure we could keep you?"

"No?"

"I had to meet with the lawyer about custody and guardianship, and was trying to balance that with arrangements for Dad," he explains. "I was getting overwhelmed and the morning of the really big meeting, Chase left me a binder of testimonials from people all around town about how we'd be the best option for you, if that was your preference."

"And who do you think helped your best friend with that project because you were too busy being a pain-in-the-ass who thought he had to handle everything himself?" Chuck asks.

I look around the table to see Chuck, Tommy, and Bryant raise their hands, all wearing the same expression telling Jax he was a fool for not figuring that out earlier.

It seems like I'm not the only one who missed out on what everyone was up to back then.

"I'll admit that I could have been a whole lot better about communicating," Jax admits.

Bryant snorts. "That's putting it mildly."

"I apologized more than once to you," Jax says.

"Yeah, for cussing me out when I told you that we were all here to help and that you didn't have to do it all on your own."

"What else did I do?"

Chuck raises his hand like we're in class. "Besides being one cranky son-of-a-bitch when you moved back into the main house?"

What the hell is happening here?

"Oh my God, it's not like you were behaving," Tommy chimes in, swatting Chuck. "You had half the house booby-trapped with pranks."

"Stop, please. I didn't mean to bring all of this stuff up. Let's just finish lunch," I say, not feeling hungry anymore after all the trouble I just caused.

Jax's hand falls on my wrist and I concentrate on keeping my hand where it is. "Matt, all of this is shit we've clearly been keeping in for a long time. Not one of us was in a good place after Dad died." He looks at our three brothers. "But you belong here with us, that's what we were trying to say before we got a little sidetracked. If you ever want or need anything different, we'll support you. But this is our home, and it would have ripped our hearts out if you had gone to live with Mom."

I glance around the table to see everyone nodding in agreement.

"No one is required to live in the main house. You can build your dream home in that plot across the stream, just don't let Tommy use the nail gun and everything will be fine."

"Seriously, when am I going to live that down?" Tommy protests. "That was one time when I was thirteen and Bryant didn't tell me it was empty or I would have never tried to secure the shingles like that."

The tightness leaves my chest as we all laugh at the memory of a gust of wind blowing off an entire row of shingles that Tommy thought he had secured along the long roof of the stables.

I drop one hand into my lap, squeezing the one that stayed put during this whole ordeal.

Chapter 48
Caleb

"Cay, are you ready?" Matt calls down from the loft.

I frantically finish typing out three more ingredients before shoving my phone back into my pocket. Immediately, I feel guilty because I can see his muscles straining, holding the rope in one hand to keep the bale in the air and not crushing me.

"Sorry," I tell him, getting a grunt in return. "Lower it down."

The stables are at-capacity and a few of the horses on this end are new to the facility so they don't need to see or hear a sixty-pound bale of straw fall from the ceiling. Yesterday, when we were fooling around in the loft, he noticed some mold on the end of this one so we decided to take a break up here after lunch today and make a show of finding it before hauling it down and having someone ask how we knew about it.

Was all of that a little stupid and over the top? Sure, but it keeps things less stressful for getting caught, especially after how emotional lunch turned out to be.

I didn't see the brothers until a few weeks after their dad passed because I was out of state for the circuit, but now I wish I had come back for the funeral. I'm not sure what I could have done, but maybe I could have helped rather than sending flowers and arranging for a few dinners to be delivered afterward.

The bale reaches my hands and I grab the two strings when it's low enough, telling Matt to let the rope drop so I can carry it outside to the wheelbarrow. This one hasn't been used this afternoon for mucking out stalls so there's plenty of space for straw.

I only have to wait a moment before I hear the click of a familiar pair of boots behind me. Matt pulls out his utility knife, slicing one string and then the other so we can shake the straw in the tray.

"I have a couple of errands to run, mind if I duck out soon?" I ask, keeping my tone casual.

Matt's forehead wrinkles as he frowns, spreading out the clumps. "Didn't we just pick up a bunch of stuff two days ago?"

Voices carry over to us from inside the stables, reminding me we're not alone and I should get moving.

"Yeah, but I forgot to take care of a couple of things around town."

What the hell am I saying?

I lift the handles of the wheelbarrow, loving the feel of my callouses fully returning, and steer it to where the soiled straw from the stalls gets stored temporarily.

"Do you want a hand?" I'm not sure if he's asking about the errands I'm trying to keep secret, or the task at-hand.

"I want you to be free this evening and ready for me to pick you up," I say in lieu of any direct answer.

"Free for what?" he prods, walking half a step behind me, hands in his pockets.

"Just don't eat dinner before I get you, okay?"

"What time are you coming back?"

"Before Tommy has the rice cooked for dinner," I say, getting more and more used to their cooking rotation. "Tell him you're eating out."

"Where, exactly, will I be eating?"

Why does his voice have to be so damn sexy? All these questions should be annoying me, especially since I'm evading half of them and need to get us on another subject before he figures things out.

Thankfully, we're at the right spot for me to tip out the straw and I make a show of checking that there isn't anything left before backing up.

"Hey, there's Gerald," I say, pointing to the half-wolf trotting around the far end of the stables.

I don't have to look at Matt to know he's skeptical of my avoidance and clear change of subject, but he humors me, giving one sharp whistle for the massive dog. He tips his head our way and runs towards us, his pink tongue lolling out the side of his open mouth.

"What have you been up to?" Matt asks, holding out his arm so Gerald can put his huge paws on it to look in his eyes.

It freaked me out the first time I met Bryant's part-feral pet. I thought he was going to tackle me or something, but it's his way of greeting someone. His tail wags happily as he sniffs Matt's shirt and then looks expectantly at me. I follow suit and, sure enough, he stands on his back legs to look at me, his tail still going back and forth. Once he's back on all fours, we pet him, his fur shedding into our hands since the weather continues to get warmer.

The dog's ears perk and he tears off towards one of the trails, probably chasing some small game.

"Well," Matt says while watching him run off, "why don't you head out now and I'll take care of this. Then you can text me when you're on your way back, and maybe give me some hint for where we're going?"

I let him take the wheelbarrow. "Just your regular clothes will do."

Then I tap him on the shoulder, wanting to do a whole lot more to say goodbye, and jog to my truck before he can ask anything else. Once my key is in the ignition and the engine roars to life, I check the list on my phone and add cider to it. Satisfied, I turn on the radio to the local country station, cranking up the tunes and rolling down the windows.

The drive to and from the ranch is becoming second nature to me and the familiar stretch of highway is comforting. Even pulling into the parking lot of the grocery store feels more and more home-like. It doesn't take me long to get everything I need from here and I'm pretty proud that I didn't have to double-back for items in aisles I already went through.

My memory still pisses me off regularly, especially when meeting people, but I get the cashier's name right before I even look at her name tag.

It feels like a massive win.

When I stop at the cafe, Sarah is ready to take my order and asks me how I'm doing and what's new at the ranch. It makes me feel seen and known in a way that I've craved for years.

Sure, I'm recognized more often than not with the rodeo being such a big deal around here, but people are getting to know *me* and not just greeting the champion bull rider. And I love it.

Back at my place, I shower all the grime off my skin from a hard day's work before staring at my closet. I know I told Matt he should wear his regular clothes, but I'm actually a little nervous all of a sudden. I have butterflies in my stomach thinking about picking him up for a date.

His brothers won't think twice about us going somewhere together, but this is going to be different. I'd like to bring him flowers, but that would be pretty obvious to everyone, so I deleted it from my list each time I put it on. Which was a few.

Finally, I opt for a snug black T-shirt and jeans that I've seen him check me out in.

"That wasn't so hard now, was it?" I mumble to myself while buckling my belt.

I rummage through my bedside table to grab a couple of supplies and pull down my thick quilts and extra pillows before heading to the kitchen to prepare the food, starting with roasting the chicken breasts. By the time those are done, everything else is ready and in the fridge. I tent some tin foil over the chicken, just like Matt likes to do, letting it sit for several minutes while I pack everything into a couple of insulated bags. Once the chicken is sliced and in a container to keep warm, it's time to go over my checklist one final time to make sure I'm not forgetting something.

As much as I'm annoyed by triple checking things, I've found it much better to get things right in the end, so my frustration is lessening with each new list I return to. And I want everything to be correct this evening. I don't want a repeat of my burned soup...even though it led to Matt leading meal prep with me.

I check off the final item on the list: text Matt.

Caleb: On my way.

Matt: What can I bring?

Caleb: Just yourself.

I put my phone in my pocket. It takes two trips to bring everything to my truck. Once the windows are down, I get on the road, feeling excited.

When I'm on the highway, I notice a whistling sound and check to see if a back window of the cab is cracked open. But everything appears to be as it usually is. I slow down, getting ready to pull over, and the sound disappears. As I increase my speed again, it starts back up, so it must be something with my engine. I pick a slower speed, closer to what I drive in town, and let people pass me, so I don't push my luck and blow something that will be too much to repair. The thought of getting rid of this truck doesn't sit well with me. It was my ticket out of my old life. The rodeo gave me a career, but to be able to do that, I needed to get there.

By the time I pull into my regular spot outside of the garage, Matt is sitting on the front porch. I momentarily forget about checking to see if something is loose because he's so damn handsome in his flannel shirt, the sleeves rolled up to his elbows.

Chapter 49
Matt

Caleb waves at me, but I'll admit that I'm confused. I thought he was picking me up, but he parked where he usually does and got out of his truck. He pops the hood though and things start to make sense.

"What happened?" I ask, jogging the rest of the way to see how I can help.

"There was a whistling sound on the highway when I was driving back," he explains. "When I decreased my speed, it went away, but each time I increased it again, the sound came back."

"When did it start?" I ask. I'm not a mechanic, but we've all gotten pretty good with figuring out an issue.

"I didn't hear it in town and it wasn't happening this morning." He thinks for a moment. "But I played music on the way into town, so it could have started then, or when I was coming back."

Listening to my gut, I go into the garage and grab a creeper. Caleb is still poking around his engine when I slide under the truck. Sure enough, I see the culprit and come back out.

"Cay, come down here," I call, getting off the creeper and offering him a hand down. He takes it and the contact feels electric as usual. "Go under and look to your right and tell me what you see."

He follows my instructions and when I hear, "What the hell?" I know he's figured it out.

"Need a knife for the zip-ties?" I ask, holding mine within reach for him.

"Who puts a harmonica under someone's truck?" he asks, taking the knife and rolling a little farther under.

"I'll give you one guess," I say, chuckling.

"Oh my God, it was your brother," he groans.

"Bingo," I sing. "You've officially made it on Chuck's list of people to prank."

Come to think of it, he's been laying off pranking me since Caleb was injured. It seems oddly thoughtful of him. I'm guessing that I'm fair game again since he's messing with Caleb now.

My secret boyfriend slides out from under his truck, his shirt riding up on one side giving me a peek at his flexed abs as he begins to sit up. I reach down and he takes my hand so I can haul him up. When he's standing, his thumb traces a small circle on the back of my hand and the intimacy of the moment hits me, bringing on that tightness and tension. I close my eyes briefly to try to relax a little, telling myself that this is okay and that I'm safe with him.

I hope.

Caleb must sense what I'm going through because he gently releases my hand.

"Remind me to tell your brother he's a dick," he says, smirking.

"You wouldn't be the first person," I say, chuckling.

I only realize now that he's not wearing his hat. His curls are loose and fall over his forehead just right. Fighting the urge to run my fingers through them, I grab the creeper and bring it back into the garage. As I'm hanging it up, I hear the hood of Caleb's truck slam closed. He's in the driver's seat when I come back out, waving to some of the workers leaving for the evening. I follow suit and hop into the passenger side, taking off my hat and putting it in the backseat.

"Will you grab that?" he asks, nodding towards something folded up on the dash in front of me.

I unwrap it, revealing a paisley pattern. "Why do we need a bandana?"

"It's for you to tie over your eyes so you can't see where we're going."

I look down at the fabric in my hands and then back at him. "You want me to wear a blindfold?"

"Yes."

"Why?" I ask when I realize he's not giving me more of an explanation.

"Because the location for our dinner is part of the surprise." He has a stubborn set to his jaw and I have a strong suspicion that I'm not going to get anything else out of him.

Folding up the bandana, I cover my eyes and tie a knot behind my head.

"No guarantees about how well it's tied. You've seen my apron," I mutter.

"It looks good to me," he says cheerily, reversing out of his spot and then driving forward. It feels like we're going down the main driveway, which seems odd.

Why couldn't I see that?

I assume we're going into Greenstone when he turns right onto the first country highway, but after that, we need to turn left to go south. Caleb seems to make a U-turn. Thankfully, he slowed down plenty and I'm not feeling like a ragdoll being tossed around.

"Please don't tell me we're lost," I groan out.

"Nope, just having some fun on the way."

I reach across the center console until I find his leg, squeezing his thigh. It's not that I don't trust him, but it's disorienting to be blindfolded, so having that contact feels good.

After a little longer, he makes another extra-long turn, throwing me off even more. At this point, I've accepted that I'm truly along for the ride and won't get any more answers, so I decide to inch my hand up his leg.

"Matt, what are you doing?" he asks.

"I'm just having some fun on the way, too," I reply, rubbing over his crotch and feeling him harden under my touch.

"Jesus, you're going to make me pull over if you keep doing that." He groans like this pains him as he grabs my wrist, moving it back to his thigh. "I promise that we can do all this and more after dinner."

"And more?" I ask, my attention piqued.

"Ah," he begins, and I want to see if he's blushing. "Without any expectations, I may have brought lube."

"I'll behave," I say without even thinking about it.

He chuckles and says, "Good to know."

We haven't spent another full night together since that first one and we've been pretty desperate whenever we're alone, one of us usually dropping to our knees within a minute. But I've been dreaming about sinking deep into him for a long time.

A very long time.

"What's your preference?" I ask, feeling both disconnected since I can't see him but also a little free not overanalyzing whatever he's doing.

"I'm mostly a bottom, if that answers your question."

I squeeze his leg again. "It does."

With that, I spend the next few minutes fantasizing about what we're going to be doing soon.

I'm still trying to picture what his face is going to look like as I push into him for the first time when he turns onto a gravel road and asks me to roll up my window. Thankfully, I've ridden in this truck often enough, I can easily find the hand crank to do that.

"Why aren't we stopping?" I ask, confused why we needed to roll up the windows.

"Someone's getting nosy once more."

"Well, you're not the one blindfolded with no idea where we are."

"You'll see soon enough. Just relax and enjoy the mystery for now."

The road gets bumpier and the sounds are muted with the windows up. When we finally park, he sets me up with music and asks me to stay put.

I can't make out what he's doing, but I can tell he's in the bed of the truck at times by the way the vehicle occasionally sways. The air smells familiar with a little more pine on the breeze than by the main house, so I don't think he drove in circles only to bring me back there.

True to his word, just before the end of the second song, another one I love, he's opening my door and turning off the music.

"Keep it on while I walk you to the right spot, please."

"Since you asked so nicely."

What can another minute blindfolded hurt at this point?

When my boots hit the ground, I can tell we're in a place with tall grass. I listen carefully for any noises that might give me a hint of where we are. But I can't hear any horses, cattle, cars, or conversations. The only sounds are a few birds chirping and the breeze blowing through the trees and grass.

"Alright, you can take it off."

Reaching to the knot at the back of my head, I make quick work of untying it and removing the bandana. Immediately, the sun feels comically bright, but I should have expected that with how long I was wearing this thing. It doesn't matter that I can barely see, I know exactly where we are: the plot where I'm going to build my house one day.

I turn around to ask him why we're here, but behind me is the bed of his pickup. And it looks positively lavish.

There are several fluffy blankets laid out to cover the whole thing and a few pillows in the back. An extra-thick cutting board is in the center with food spread out and two hard ciders ready to drink.

I look at him, about to ask what all this is for, but he shrugs before I get anything out and says, "Today was a really big deal and it seemed right to celebrate with a proper date."

I'm stunned speechless.

Chapter 50
Caleb

Matt watches me, his eyes getting misty before he swipes at them.

"I know lunch wasn't easy and a lot of truths came out that seemed to surprise everyone, but I wanted to make sure you got to visit the site of your future home."

He looks out across the landscape, taking in the field in front of us with rolling hills beyond, then the forest surrounding us with the mountains in the background. He turns to face me once more, taking a few steps and then reaching out his hand.

His fingers trail down my bare skin starting at my elbow, his eyes following their progress. Still saying nothing, he interlocks our fingers, lifting the back of my hand to his lips. They're soft and linger against my skin for a moment before he lowers our hands, fingers still intertwined.

"Thank you," he whispers.

Part of me wants to brush it off as no big deal, but that would minimize the importance of what we're celebrating.

"You're welcome," I reply instead.

"What made you give me the note?" he asks quickly, like he's been wanting to know for some time.

I'm a little surprised by the question.

"I guess I needed to know for sure if there was any sort of chance of being with you."

He hums a sound of understanding but leaves it at that.

"What would you have done if I hadn't been standing there when you read it?" I ask, not realizing that was something I'd been curious about.

"Probably would have gone to find you, been interrupted by several people along the way, and by the time I saw you, I'd have gotten it in my head that your note meant something else."

"So you might not have done anything?"

"Let's just be thankful you were there and I didn't have time to stew, panic, and overthink things," he says, tugging on my hand and pulling me in for a hug.

"I'm thankful for you every damn day, Matthew," I say into the crook of his neck.

"I'm thankful for you, too."

It's my turn to tug on his hand, steering him to the open tailgate. "Get in."

He uses the bumper as a step to get into the bed of the truck without rocking it much. Then he gently maneuvers around to one side of the cutting board and I take the other.

"You made all of this?" he asks, taking it all in.

"Everything but the chips and the tortillas, but we can make them sometime when I get a new press."

"Really?" He sounds impressed and that's making me blush a little.

"I may have flubbed a bit about my cooking skills in some areas," I admit. "Dig in."

"You said you needed a new press?"

"Tortilla press," I explain. "I had one for years that broke a few months before I got injured and I hadn't gotten around to replacing it."

"Oh my God, this is delicious," he says, crunching a chip piled with the salsa I prepared. "Are those mango chunks in there?"

I nod. "I was lucky they were ripe at the store, otherwise, you'd probably have peach salsa. Mango is always better though."

"What's on the chicken?" he asks, putting some onto his tortilla.

"My Tex-Mex spice mix, which you won't mock once you taste it."

He adds peppers, lettuce, shredded carrots, salsa, cilantro, and avocado before accepting a lime wedge to squeeze over the top. When he takes a bite, he closes his eyes and groans.

"How did I not know you cooked like this?"

I smile, putting the finishing touches on my tacos. "I never really make these for other people. Whenever someone comes over, I just order food, and when you'd visit, we usually went out to eat. It's probably been five months since I last made any of this."

"I strongly request you don't go that long before you make it again," he says, taking a swig of his hard cider. "I'll warn you, if you make this for my brothers, they'll likely demand you officially join the cooking rotation."

The idea of bringing something to the table at Landen Acres warms me from the inside. Of being wanted for something I enjoy doing.

It's not long before we've eaten our fill, and we work together to clear away everything from the meal. I shut the door after getting the last of it into the back seat and start to turn around, only to be caged in by two strong arms. Matt's nose runs up the back of my neck causing me to shiver even though it's plenty warm outside.

"Can I help you with anything?" I manage, my hands reaching behind me to pull his hips against me. When his bulge is pressed over my ass, he nips at my earlobe and I let out a gasp.

"You mentioned you brought something special along when I was," he flicks my ear with his tongue, "exploring you in the car."

"I didn't have any expectations," I say, not wanting to pressure him into anything.

One of his hands leaves the truck and he presses his palm against my abs, grinding against me. "Well, if you're interested, I definitely am."

"Glove compartment," I wheeze, starting to lose rational thought with him surrounding me like this, need practically dripping from his voice.

"I'll meet you in the back of your truck in a moment, and I hope you'll have your boots off." With that, the heat from his chest leaves and he hops into the driver's seat, leaning over to reach the glove compartment.

I hustle to the truck bed, pulling off my boots right when I sit down. Even with my haste, I've only just removed my second one when he's taking it from my grasp and tugging me by my knees to the edge of the tailgate, bringing his lips to mine in a searing kiss that takes my breath away.

God, I didn't realize how badly I'd been missing this side of him. Even if we were telling everyone about us, *this* would still be mine. The unbridled way he lets go with me is even better than I imagined.

My fingers are frantic on his shirt as I work the top buttons free, knowing that if I were to yank it open, he'd have to explain what happened to his brothers. We're both pulling up at the same time, desperate to touch each other, tossing our shirts somewhere in the truck bed.

Before I can kiss him again, Matt is already working his mouth down my neck and chest, pressing one hand to my sternum so I'm leaning back on my elbows. While he's paying special attention to one of my nipples, he unbuckles my belt and undoes my jeans, stroking me over my underwear.

"No fair," I gasp out. "You still have your boots on."

He pauses and looks up at me with those blue eyes, his broad chest expanding with each deep breath.

"I wouldn't want to play unfairly." He licks my nipple with the flat of his tongue and an embarrassingly strangled sound escapes me. "Why don't you slip out of those while I join you?"

I don't have to be told twice as I shimmy out of my jeans and boxer briefs while scooting back onto the padding of the blankets. He makes quick work of undressing, setting his boots and the rest of his clothes on the tailgate. He pulls out the bottle of lube I brought from one of his pockets and steps up into the bed, his dick finally coming into view.

My mouth waters at the sight of him naked in front of me. His tan lines will continue to get more pronounced as the summer wears on, but right now, he's just-sun-kissed and his freckles are multiplying. He crawls over me, forcing me to lay back against the pillows

His lips are on mine again and I can taste the sweetness from the cider when his tongue sweeps into my mouth. Fingers thread through my hair and he groans against me as he settles his weight on top of me, our bodies pressing into one another.

"Tell me how to prep you," he whispers between kisses.

"I'm sure whatever you're used to will be good," I reply, lost in the sensation of how he's all-consuming.

He lifts his chest and face, and I assume it's to open the lube but he's hesitating. I try to wrap my mind around what it could be, but nothing comes to mind.

"That might not be so helpful," he says.

Having his length rubbing against mine isn't *helpful* for having a coherent response.

"As long as I'm prepped, I'm good to go," I pant. "I can do it if you don't like to."

"I want to," he says with determination.

Why is he being so odd?

"But um," he says, looking nervous, "you should probably walk me through this so I don't mess anything up."

"Have you done this before?" I ask, not fully sure if I spoke the words out loud until he winces ever so slightly.

"No," he replies, which I can see is making him a little uncomfortable. I try to process past my shock at this being his first time. The fact that I'm the one he's going to experience this with is definitely something I'm going to enjoy.

I had no idea my boyfriend was new to this.

"We'll go slow, don't worry," I reassure him.

He raises an eyebrow at me. "Going slow isn't necessary," he says, his hand running up the inside of my thigh. "I just don't want to do it wrong and hurt you."

I point to the lube. "Plenty of that," I say, trying to be helpful but his fingers cradle my sack as I attempt to think. "Start with one finger and slowly add more."

His hand leaves me and he pops the bottle open, coating his index finger. Pushing my knee up to my chest with his elbow, I do the same with the other, exposing me to him as he paints the excess lube where he'll be pushing into soon. I watch as he's completely focused on the task at hand, his mouth falling open when he watches the tip of his finger disappear.

"Fuck, that's so sexy," he says, his voice husky and full of need.

Chapter 51
Matt

He's so damn tight and it's just the tip of my finger.

I know he'll be able to relax and take me, but holy shit, I wasn't expecting *this*.

Pulling my hand away, I generously coat more of my fingers with lube before capping the bottle and leaning over him, pressing one of his thighs against his chest. I kiss him just as my first finger penetrates him, slowly working its way in and out. His hands hold me tightly as his tongue finds mine.

He tastes like my favorite hard cider this evening, making it even more perfect. I'm still amazed that this man wants *me*.

My finger moves smoothly now so I press a second digit at his entrance.

"Yes," he says against my mouth and I add that in, keeping my rhythm steady and smooth.

"Scissor them," he instructs between kisses, and I add some separation, hoping that's what he means.

He gives an enthusiastic nod as if he can read me and I keep pumping, not sure if I should be changing anything to hit his prostate just yet.

"And a third."

I let out a curse as I feel him slowly relax around my fingers, accepting them and knowing that soon I'll be seated deep inside him. Part of me is already curious to have him finger me because watching how he reacts to just this has me so turned on.

He gently cups the side of my face and I pull back a little. "Are you ready?"

"Are you?" I ask in reply, pumping my fingers again.

"Matt, I've been ready for you for a long time," he says earnestly, making me feel more sure that he can take me now.

I kiss him once more and give his lower lip a light bite before sitting up and reaching for the lube again. My hands have a slight tremor to them, not because I'm nervous, but because I've wanted this so badly and I can't fully believe where I am.

"Where do you want me?" he asks, his feet on the blanket.

"Just like that," I say, not having to think about my response. "I want to be able to watch your expression the whole time."

He gives me a slow, sexy grin as I make sure I'm well-lubed. I put a little more on my fingertip and rub it onto his puckered hole. Lifting one of his legs so his ankle is on my shoulder, I get into position while he pulls his other leg back.

The tip of my dick rests against his hole as I grip the base and look at him. He nods and I press forward, rocking and pushing until my head makes it in.

"Fuck, you're tight," I moan.

"Keep going," he says, almost whimpering with need.

I thrust shallowly so I don't hurt him and it feels like I'm pressing through a tight tunnel until I get past those muscles. Watching more and more of my shaft disappear is mesmerizing. We go carefully, but it's not long until I'm fully seated, loving the way he feels around me and watching his dick leak precum already.

Wiping the lube I got on my hand onto the blanket, I grab Caleb's free hand and bring it above his head, keeping our fingers entwined. He looks a little surprised at my choice but doesn't say anything. Something about this feels more vulnerable than what we've done so far, and even more vulnerable than what I've done with other people. I want to feel my connection with him and I want him to see what he means to me.

My hips pull back and push forward until they're pressed against his ass once more. I repeat the motion, getting used to the concentrated tightness anal offers that I haven't experienced before.

It's safe to say that I fucking love it.

It seems like my boyfriend is enjoying himself as well, but I know something isn't quite right so I shift my hips slightly to change the angle of how I'm entering him.

This time when I thrust, he cries out, his hand squeezing mine as his muscles contract around me, and I know I've hit his prostate. My hips start moving on their own accord as I watch every response his body has as our pleasure builds.

As much as I want to see what we're doing, the need to connect *more* with him is almost overwhelming. I keep this pace and devour his moans in a bruising kiss, my tongue sweeping into his mouth.

I've never felt this strongly for anyone before and this connection seems like it could swallow me whole. I'm sure I'll be terrified later when I unpack all of this, but right now, something unlocks deep inside of me, tethering me to this moment and to this man. Something that I've kept locked away.

Sweat drips down my back and my movements become a little more frantic.

"I'm close," I whisper against his lips. "Where should—"

"Don't pull out," he says, gasping as I hit his prostate again. "If you touch me, I'll be coming with you."

"Fuck yes," I say, lifting up the arm most of my weight was on and repositioning myself so I can move that hand between us.

My fingers wrap around his girth, and he moans into my mouth as his muscles clench around me so tightly that my rhythm breaks. I shudder from the increased pressure and try to focus on us peaking together. My thumb rubs over his tip, swiping the precum over his head. He twitches underneath me and he lifts himself to close the small distance between our mouths, kissing me hard. His breath comes out hot against my face as I stroke him to the same pace my hips are setting.

I try to draw things out for both of us, but that tingling sensation surprises me with how quickly it hits, my balls tightening almost immediately.

"Cay," I say in a warning.

"Don't stop," he almost whines, desperation lacing his voice.

My grip around him tightens as I crush our lips together, grunting as my orgasm hits. It takes a concentrated effort to keep stroking him while I'm coming deep inside of him, slamming as tightly as I can against his ass. Before I'm finished, warmth hits my fingers and he's right there with me, groaning, twitching, and practically choking my dick.

I'm not sure that I've ever come that hard.

I slide out of Caleb and collapse onto my back next to him while he relaxes his legs.

"Fuck, that was amazing," I say, out of breath and reaching across to pull him against me.

He's so relaxed, it's easy to have him nuzzle his face against my shoulder and wrap his body around mine, using me as a pillow.

"You're telling me," he says, sounding fully sated. "I was seeing stars at the end."

I'll admit that hearing that warms my pride as I lace my fingers with his over my chest, noting that there's no tightness. No panic.

Just a sense of calm and rightness as we lay together.

"Can you initiate holding my hand when we're in the truck driving back?" I ask after a bit. "Don't tell me before though."

The tip of his thumb lightly rubs along the bottom side of mine in a comforting way.

"Are you sure?" he asks.

"Yeah, it'll be a good way for me to expect it without knowing when it's coming."

"What happens if I don't let go between now and when we get back to the main house?" On anyone else that might sound sassy, but from him, it almost sounds like a challenge.

"Not possible," I counter. "Unless we're not putting our shirts back on."

"That's too bad," he says, shifting a little and making me realize how sweaty we got.

"Which one? That we have to put our shirts back on or that we can't keep holding hands the whole time?"

He shrugs a shoulder and says, "Both," making me smile.

"Can I ask you something?" he asks before tilting his head and kissing my chest, sending tingles through me.

"Yeah."

"What was new for you today?" His words seem carefully chosen, like he's been figuring out how to ask it.

"Everything after I popped the cap off the bottle," I answer honestly.

His thumb pauses its motion and he looks up at me. "I should have checked with—"

"Nope, I'm going to stop you right there," I interrupt. "You gave me the guidance I needed. As long as you tell me if I'm doing anything uncomfortable, that's the biggest thing."

"You're sure?"

"I'm sure," I say, kissing his forehead. "It was amazing, I already told you that."

"Is there anything else that would be a new experience for you?"

"Caleb," I reply, ready to get it out in the open, not that it was a secret, "everything with you has been a new experience."

He's quiet as he processes this information.

"Not true." It's a simple response but one that leaves me confused.

"Excuse me?"

"There's no way I was the first person you gave a blow job to."

I bark out a laugh. "What is that supposed to mean?"

"I've gotten enough to know when someone hasn't done it before," he says, giving me a skeptical look.

"Well that's a damn relief because I didn't want it to suck for you."

"Oh you sucked all right," he says with a shit-eating grin on his face before we both laugh.

After a little while, we quiet down and I eventually flip some of the blanket over us as we look out at the view. As I lie here with Caleb in my arms, in the place I'm going to build a home, I can't help but hope it could be a home for us.

Chapter 52
Caleb

Two weeks later

Tommy pulls the notebook and pen from this pocket and hands it to his girlfriend, Sam. She beams up at him and quickly flips to an open page to write down a couple of ideas she and Avery thought of.

"Rebecca mentioned something about a new insurance option, too, so we should ask her whenever she can come by next to talk," Avery says, causing Sam to nod and write faster.

They've been working hard on a co-op idea to make care more affordable for the ranchers and farmers in the area, hoping to find a system that could help other rural areas.

I set the veggie tray out with two different dips that Matt and I made earlier today on either side of it. As I make my way back to the kitchen, I see Jackson sit down on the end of the bigger couch, pulling Avery onto his lap. She gives a squeak of surprise but settles right into what seems to be her favorite place.

It's times like these where it feels a lot harder to just be hanging out with my best friend and pretend like he isn't so much more than that. We've gotten to the point where he's not panicking when I hold his hand, but we only do that in private. I think he's feeling more ready to try something soon, to see if that triggers any panicked response.

But being automatically invited and part of the group feels pretty amazing. It makes me think that I made the right choice in leasing the apartment in Greenstone.

No one is in the kitchen when I enter except for Matt, who is pouring the homemade caramel into the dish in the center of a plate with sliced apples. I know everyone else is busy in the other room, so I take a risk and slip my arm around his waist from behind and kiss the back of his neck. He lets out a soft moan just before I release him.

"You're staying here tonight, right?" he asks.

Tommy was the one to suggest I not only leave clothes here, but to stay in one of the unused bedrooms whenever I want. So it hasn't been too hard to pretend that I'm sleeping in the room next to Matt's. No one seems to have caught on that I'm actually spending the night in Matt's bed yet.

"I could be persuaded," I reply.

He gets that look in his eyes that tells me he's ready to be very persuasive just before Chuck comes into the kitchen, going right to the fridge. He pulls out four bottles of his favorite beer and closes the door.

"I thought everyone had drinks already," I comment.

Chuck gives me a resigned look. "They do. These are for me to get through the movie without complaining."

"Not a fan of rom-coms, I take it?"

He gives an exaggerated shudder. "Not in the least."

"You're a good man to support Tommy's selection then," I say, chuckling.

"I am," he agrees, going out to likely claim his favorite chair.

Grabbing the giant bowl of popcorn, my own beer, and the stack of plates for everyone to use, I find myself pinned against the counter from behind with very-familiar lips tugging at my earlobe. As quickly as he trapped me, Matt is off to the sink to soak the caramel pot like nothing happened.

"Just how bad am I blushing?" I ask, turning around.

He looks over his shoulder with a wink. "The room is already darkened for the movie, you'll be fine."

I roll my eyes and take a centering breath, willing myself to not have tented pants from that small interaction. It's futile because any contact with Matt has me ready to go with how much sneaking around we've been doing.

"Are you all good without your glasses?"

"Yes, chef," I reply, knowing he's referring to my blue light glasses. It's been freeing to not need them.

Courtney comes in through the front door as I leave the kitchen and she immediately hops over to me, moving locks of my hair to the side. "We should get you in again so I can clean this up."

I can't help but smile. Since she volunteered at the auction, she's become the expert on my hair and there's something about her lack of filter that I find refreshing. "Let me know when you can squeeze me in and I'll make it work."

"You're a good man, Caleb," she says with a smile before she practically skips to the sofa where her girlfriends are still in planning mode. "No, this is movie night. We're done talking about work."

I can't help but smile at the double-standard since she just talked about work with me as I follow behind.

"You made it," Avery squeals, jumping off Jax's lap and hugging her while Sam visibly panics between finishing her notes and doing the same.

"Finish writing," Courtney says from over Avery's head.

Tommy looks back at the door as I set things on the coffee table and take a seat with my beer on the smaller sofa. "Just you tonight?"

She gives a rueful smile. "Just me."

Avery hugs her tighter. "It's time to let this guy go, he's clearly not worth it."

Sam gives her a sympathetic smile as she joins the hug while Tommy nods from his seat. "You can't let him drag you along like this."

Courtney sighs, clearly having heard this from everyone before. "It's all going to change soon. I know it doesn't look good right now, but things are out of his hands for a little bit longer than expected."

"Is this guy in the mafia or something?" Chuck asks, already half a beer into his bottles.

"She's not telling us any details until they've had a proper date," Tommy explains, rolling his eyes.

"What makes this guy so different?" I ask.

Courtney freezes and quickly glances at Tommy before sitting down between Sam and Avery, who is back on Jax's lap. "Um, that will be revealed if things work out."

I look at Tommy. "Is it always like this?"

"Never," he replies. "Which is why we're chomping at the bit to know who this damn guy is and why she's allowed him to *not* show up for over a month."

She sighs. "It's complicated."

"Not really," Tommy says.

"You deserve so much more than someone who won't be seen in public with you," Sam says sincerely, resting her hand on Courtney's knee.

Ouch, that hit a little close to home.

"It's not like that, really," Courtney says. "If I say more, you'll know who it is and we want a chance to know if this is something before that happens."

It's not until Courtney is done defending herself that I notice Matt's listening. He's standing stock-still just outside the kitchen with the apple tray in his hands, staring at me, looking torn.

I give him a small smile and nod, letting him know that I'm okay with us taking our time. We don't need to be rushing into something that can affect more than just the two of us. That seems to shake him out of his stupor and he brings the tray to the table without joining the conversation.

"Enough about me," Courtney proclaims. "There are other single people in this room to grill next."

Matt lets out a cough and mutters something about needing to get a cider and retreating back to the kitchen.

"Caleb," Chuck sings. I can see Matt's back tense just before he disappears around the corner to get his drink. "I haven't seen you go out with anyone since you've moved here. Spill."

Grateful for the shades being closed and fewer lights on for the movie because I'm blushing, I say the first thing I can think that wouldn't tip them all off.

"You just said you haven't seen me go out with anyone." I make sure I smirk before I take a sip of my beer. "So there can't be anything to spill, unfortunately."

He tips the neck of the bottle towards me. "I don't buy it. Not when you're probably the only person in this town with more charm than me."

Bryant, Tommy, and Jax all groan.

"What? Y'all know it's true," he says, catching the pillow Tommy throws at him and tucking it behind his head. "So?"

"Everyone here knows I've been on a date," I say, knowing full well I'm being a snot.

Chuck rolls his eyes. "That would only count if you saw Cora again."

Unfortunately, I don't have any other thoughts on how to evade saying I'm seeing someone without lying to everyone in the room. I take another drink to buy myself time.

When I open my mouth, I truly do not know what words might come out. But I'm cut off as a hand comes from behind me to grab my jaw and pulls my face so I would be looking up at the ceiling.

Would be, but all I see are two icy blue eyes staring at me as the face I want to wake up next to every day is quickly closing in. Before I can process what's going on, Matt's lips crash with mine, his tongue swiping at the seam of my mouth, demanding access.

My free hand grabs the back of his neck as he claims me in front of his family, holding on like my life depends on it and trying hard not to moan.

Chapter 53
Matt

I'm on Caleb like a man possessed, *needing* him to know that hiding him is the last thing I wanted. Because we're past the point of backing out and everything being okay. At least I am.

God, these past few weeks have been glimpses into what I could have and I've been letting my hangups keep the best thing that's ever happened to me a secret.

There's a muted sound in his throat that I can feel better than I can hear because there are people reacting to this show of affection they've never seen from me. His fingers grip the back of my neck like a vise as he gives just as much as he gets from me.

Finally, Chuck's loud *whoop* pulls me out of the spell. I stand but not before whispering, "I'm sorry."

Caleb looks up at me with a little confusion, his lips thoroughly kissed and his hand still holding on tight.

"For if you ever felt like I didn't want this," I clarify.

Understanding crosses his features and he tugs me back down for a quick kiss before relaxing his grip.

"Any other questions for Caleb?" I ask the group as I walk around the sofa, trying to not let reality sink in about how I outed our relationship so abruptly.

"So. Many." Of course Courtney would be ready with questions. "When did this start?"

I hold my hand out for Caleb's and give him a tug to stand. He looks a little dazed yet curious about what I'm up to. Casually, I plunk myself down in the corner, with one leg running down the cushions, and give him an expectant but hopeful look.

"Far too recently for what we both would have liked it seems," I reply, thinking about his letter once more.

He sits down so he's lounging against me, his back resting on my chest and his head on my shoulder. I drape my arm around him and a quick glance is the only warning I get before he slips his hand into mine.

The memory of panicking is there, but it's more of a reminder of how far I've come. At least that's what I try to remind myself whenever I feel guilty for how terribly that day at the rodeo went.

"Who made the first move?"

Caleb raises his beer.

"I'll give you that one because you said something first," I grumble into his ear. "But we both know I kissed you first."

"Think what you'd like, I'm still your boyfriend now, which is all that matters," he replies, quiet enough so I'm the only one who hears.

"Damn right." I nip his ear and relax back into the corner of the sofa.

Everyone is watching us.

"Did I miss something?" I whisper.

"How am I supposed to know?" he whispers right back. "My boyfriend was distracting me."

"Oh my God, I don't care they're ignoring my question because they're so fucking adorable," Courtney stage whispers.

Before either of us can ask what her question was, she's already switching gears to the movie. I take the reprieve to look at each of my brothers in turn. Bryant smiles at us while Jax gives us a nod of approval. Tommy gives us a thumbs up and Chuck mouths the words "about time."

"Do you think Chuck suspected something?" Caleb asks me, still keeping his voice low.

"I have no clue," I reply honestly. For all I know, he could be referring to the fact that I've never sat like this with anyone I was dating. Never brought them into my daily life, and definitely never to something with my whole family.

But seeing them all happy for me means the world to me.

Tommy gets the movie up on the big TV and everyone's attention goes there. Everyone's but mine. I'm not sure how much of the opening I miss because I'm trying to memorize every detail about how content I feel. The way Caleb's body relaxes against mine makes me feel more at home with someone than I ever have before.

Eventually, he looks up at me, sets our bottles on the ground, and asks what I'd like to eat.

"Just get extras on your plate and I'll be good," I say, kissing his forehead.

"I'll be right back."

He returns with a plate filled with a variety of the snacks we prepared, heavy on the veggies for me, and sitting exactly where he was earlier, practically melting against me. Much to my delight, he balances the plate on his lap, dips a carrot into our homemade red pepper hummus, and passes it back to me. I happily crunch on everything he hands me until the plate is empty and he shifts, poking a finger into my side in a silent request for me to sit up a little. His arm is tucked behind my back before he rests his cheek against my shoulder so he's curled around me more than before. Without giving it a second thought, I hold the hand that rests on my chest, and he lets out a contented sigh. We stay like this for the rest of the movie.

When the credits roll, Bryant stands and stretches. "Chuck and I are on cleanup."

"Am I being punished because I'm the only other single person here?" he asks with mock offense. "You know that it's only a matter of time before Rebecca asks me out."

A collective groan is the only response he gets.

"Please, be nice to the—" Tommy begins.

"I am," Chuck says, throwing up his hands. "How many times do I have to tell you that?"

"It's not like you've ever had to work for someone's attention before," I point out.

"Precisely," he says. "So there's no reason for any of you to think I'm going to mess things up with the new vet."

"I don't think he understood that you meant he doesn't know what he's doing," Caleb whispers to me.

"Agreed," I whisper back. "But we'll let him think I meant it in a helpful manner and slip upstairs."

Chuck continues to list off his many virtues and other attributes that will make it impossible for Rebecca Quist to not fall madly in love with him. Caleb and I quietly stand up together. When I reach for our dish and bottles, Bryant shakes his head and then nods towards the stairs.

Blushing, I take Caleb's hand in mine and lead him upstairs, getting smiles from everyone else still on the couches. Everyone except Chuck who hasn't figured out we've left because he's pulling out his phone to show off recent photos of Gertrude.

"How could anyone *not* fall in love with her?" he exclaims. "Once they've been properly introduced, she'll be coming by daily just to see Gertrude, and who will happen to be around his favorite lady?"

"You," everyone else chimes in when we reach the top of the stairs.

"Is he going to be mad we left during his persuasive speech?" Caleb asks.

"We'll probably get a recap at breakfast tomorrow since he seems set on winning her over," I say with a shrug, letting us into my bedroom.

"Your brother is relentless."

"Around us, definitely," I agree. "But so far, he's been good around her."

"He could always leave some flowers and a note at her door," he says.

I pull him into an embrace, relishing in the step we took today. "We both know that's a foolproof way to get someone's attention."

"It definitely is," he says, leaning in to kiss me.

I pull back for a second, running my hands up to cup his face, and look into his eyes.

"I love you."

It's a simple statement and not one that I've ever meant like this. But something about this moment, this night, felt right.

"Just in case you were ever unsure," he says, "I've been in love with you for quite some time, Matthew Landen."

All those doubts get pushed aside, even if they're only quiet for one night, and I'm able to be with the man of my dreams in peace.

Chapter 54
Caleb

Two months later

Cornelius Farthington, or Neal, gets smoother every time we ride. Maybe it's because we're taking his favorite trail today, I'm not sure, but we've definitely found our stride.

When I first saw him at the smaller stables where Jax works with horses with more trauma, I knew he was mine. His former owners bought him in hopes of racing him, but he was injured during training and refused to run for them, even well after he was fully healed. They did what they could, but he didn't like being around too many people, or even other horses, for that matter.

Jax worked diligently to build up his confidence and comfort, but the owners were getting antsy, so I made them an offer for Cornelius. They accepted and he's been mine ever since.

He's a gorgeous black stallion with a white patch on one leg and he runs like the damn wind. I don't even mind wearing a helmet because riding him is unlike any other horse I've been on.

Pretty soon, Scarlett's tan nose enters my peripheral vision as we're slowing down to a canter as we get closer to that beautiful little rise on the ranch. I glance back to see Matt smiling at me.

"I think you might have one of the fastest horses in the area," he calls out.

I pull on the reins so it's easier to talk before we see everyone.

"He really is something," I say, patting his neck proudly.

Honestly, I don't care about his speed. I care how connected I feel to Neal and how he seems to fit right into life here at Landen Acres.

Just like me.

"Are you sure you don't need anything else?" I ask.

"As long as you're not about to turn Neal around, then I have everything I need. And, to preemptively answer your next question, I'm still excited, just like the last time you checked in with me."

I can't seem to help it. This is such a big moment not only for Matt, but for his brothers, too, that I want to make sure there's nothing missing.

"Alright then," I say, unable to hide how happy I am that his brothers will be here for this.

Not that I doubted any of them, but having grown up with my parents, I know that familial support isn't something that I'll ever take for granted. But it's something that could have been dismissed as a silly ceremony. Instead, they're all in their places.

Our horses climb the small rise to where it flattens out and I don't look ahead at what I know is waiting for us. I look back at Matt's face as he registers the surprise we put together for him.

"You said it was just us breaking ground," he says, his eyes welling up a little.

I shrug. "They wanted to be part of this officially being yours."

"Did you do this?" he asks me.

"I just handled the logistics for making it all happen at the right time," I say, not wanting to take anything away from how important it was to each brother to be here for Matt.

It feels like it was the least I could do. He's been doing so much to support my quest in finding how I'd like to retire on top of proudly walking hand-in-hand with me everywhere, that I really wanted to surprise him with something. Hell, he even arranged for the "kiss cam" to find us at the rodeo last weekend. He went so far as distracting me so the person sitting next to him could record the big screen with Matt's phone during the kiss.

A still from that very video has been my phone's wallpaper ever since that day, much to his delight.

"Why do my brothers have shovels?" he asks quietly as we dismount and wrap our horses' reins around the post we installed earlier this summer.

"I think you could ask them," I reply.

He takes his own shovel from his saddle bag, pausing and looking confused when I hold my hand out for it.

"I'll be the only one without one," he says.

"Trust me."

He gives me the shovel their dad picked out for him when he turned fifteen, puts his hands in his pockets, and walks over to his brothers. I recently learned that each of the brothers received one that's similar for their fifteenth birthdays, but Jax, who is holding two, holds one out to Matt.

"We wanted you to use this one today for the official ground-breaking."

Avery, who is standing off to the side taking pictures with Samantha, pointedly clears her throat.

"Dad asked me to use his for breaking ground on my house, so it's only right that you do the same," he adds.

Matt looks at the well-used shovel, running his fingers over the long, wooden handle. "Are you sure?"

All four of his brothers say, "Yes," which seems to give Matt a little more confidence.

"We looked over the information you got from the engineer again and figured the house would likely be right around here," Tommy says, pointing to a stake recently pounded into the ground. "But you can dig anywhere, of course."

Matt stops about twenty paces in front of the stake, turning to look out over the fields where the cattle are grazing.

"This is where I picture the front door to be."

That's all he says before pushing the tip of the spade into the ground then stepping on the back end of the blade to bury it into the earth. Sam squeaks, rushing around everyone to get photos of Matt's face before he's done.

The brothers clap as Matt lifts a chunk of grass and dirt from the spot, tossing it away from the stake. One by one, they each make the hole a little wider, Avery and Sam capturing it all.

Matt looks expectantly at me. "Are you just going to watch or are you going to put that shovel to good use?"

Bryant, the last to contribute, takes a step back and motions for me to come over. Thankfully, no one has really said much, so I don't have to try to clear the lump in my throat and speak. Matt was under the impression that it was just the two of us going out and he'd be digging a little hole and we'd head back to make dinner for everyone. Me participating wasn't something I planned on, but I'm honored to do so.

As I press the shovel Matt's dad gave him into the ground, it feels like a statement. One that this is where I belong, and these are the people I belong to.

Chapter 55
Matt

Watching Caleb stand with my brothers feels right.

Everything with Caleb feels that way though.

"Thank you," I say to everyone. "I didn't think that you all would want to be here."

"Stop," Chuck says.

"What he means," Bryant cuts in, "is that we have some making up to do. We want to keep showing you that you've been wanted from the start."

They all nod.

"That's exactly what I was going to say," Chuck mutters.

"Uh-huh," Tommy says. Then he walks up to me and hugs me. I'm caught off guard but am able to return the embrace before we release each other.

Bryant, Chuck, and Jax follow suit. My eyes are filled by the time Jax releases me, telling me our dad would be proud of who I've become. I wipe my eyes before the waterworks open up, but I'm touched by everything.

I turn to the person who set this up, reaching for his hand and pulling him close for a kiss.

"Thank you," I whisper, just for him.

"I have to get back to the house for a video call," Avery says, coming over and hugging me, her engagement ring catching the sunlight.

Sam keeps taking pictures and it gives me an idea.

"Can you set that up so we can all be in one to hang in the house?"

"Pardon?" she asks.

"I want you and Avery in the photo, too," I explain, knowing how much she means to Tommy.

She tries to hide her surprise but sets the camera up on the back of the ATV someone drove here on. We adjust where we're standing based on her instruction before she jogs over, her bracelets jingling, and softly counts down from ten.

We take two more before people head out. Everyone seems to assume correctly that Caleb and I are going to stay for a few more minutes. Bryant even calls over his shoulder that he'd like chicken or pork tacos since we've had so much beef for dinner recently.

"We have chicken ready for the tacos, don't worry," Caleb says. He's been excited to cook for everyone regularly ever since he got his new tortilla press.

We stand in a comfortable quiet for a while, listening to the sounds of animals moving about once the truck and ATVs leave. I slip my arm around his waist, and he rests his head on my shoulder.

"Would it be presumptuous of me to," he pauses and gestures at the area we dug up and the stake, "share an opinion or two for the layout of this particular house?"

Butterflies seem to take over my gut because we haven't explicitly said this would be *our* home. I've hoped and assumed he'd be moving in with me, especially since he barely spends any time at his apartment. In fact, about a month ago, I casually offered to help him bring his clothes and other essentials out in one trip.

Actually, I'm pretty sure the only things in his fridge are spoiled now except one or two unopened cheese bricks.

"I think it would be important for you to have a say in wherever you live," I say carefully.

His mouth twitches to the side at my words. "And would this be such a place?"

With a monumental effort to not assume he's messing with me, because this man has shown me again and again he truly loves me and wants to be with me, I swallow down the mounting fear that this could somehow turn into a rejection of sorts. Instead, I dig deep for that bravery he brings out, the one that helps me be my true self, and shut down the panic.

"I'd like it to be."

"Oh thank God," he says, letting out a deep breath. "That makes all of this next piece a hell of a lot easier."

He gestures for me to sit down, right where I imagine the steps leading up to the screen porch will be, and joins me, putting his hand in mine.

"I know that your doubts still creep in at times," he says gently. "So I thought of something that might help remind you that I love you and that I'm here."

He digs a hand into his front pocket and pulls something out, hiding it in a closed fist.

"I want to be clear that this isn't a proposal, *but*," he rushes to add, "I plan to marry you one day, Matthew Landen, and the day I officially propose to you is going to be a big deal."

I'm definitely not breathing right now.

"But I got these for us," he says, opening his hand to reveal two matching rings designed with a horse's stirrup shape detail. They're stunning and simple. "They're the right size where we can either both wear them on our ring fingers or, you can put the smaller one on your pinky, and I can wear the bigger one on my middle finger. So, if you'd like to wear it, it's something that can remind you that I always want your hand in mine. It's something you can feel to ground yourself. And it's something you can see me wearing as a sign that I'm not going anywhere."

I let out a shaky breath, reaching over to touch the rings. They're warm from being in his pocket.

"Or we can put them on necklaces, or keep them on the nightstand," he adds quickly. "You don't have to wear it."

There isn't a big difference between them, but I notice there's a matching inscription on the inside of each band. It reads:

Always yours

That's what he signed the note with. When he took the chance to tell me how he felt months ago. I still read that note every damn day, placing it on top of the book where I pressed the bouquet. It won't be much longer before their frame will arrive and I can surprise him with how I preserved them.

"You're really going to propose one day?" I ask, tracing the rings in my palm.

"Without a doubt."

Nodding, I take the smaller one and slip it onto my pinky, watching how it goes on smoothly. Then I lift his hand, to find it shaking a little now, and push the larger ring onto his middle finger. Even though his response was filled with confidence, he's now the nervous one after I found my calm.

"Then these will be perfect until the day I accept," I say, finally looking into his eyes, which have sparkles of gold from the sunlight.

The spell of tension breaks as he lets out a cheer and pounces on me, tackling me to the ground and kissing me until it's time to head back to the main house to make tacos for everyone.

Acknowledgements

A book is never written in a bubble of one person and so many wonderful people were there along the way to thank!

Andra and Hayley - you two are fabulous alpha readers and your feedback makes each story stronger! Thank you!

Ashley and Tiffany - thank you so much for your beta feedback, I appreciate it so much! Thank you!Brandi - your edits make everything come together and I can't thank you enough!

Sarah - thank you for yet another gorgeous cover!

Winda - your art brings these characters to life in such beautiful ways! Thank you for all you do!

Evy - you're around for all my ideas, my tweaks, and more...it's so fun being on this journey with you!ARC readers - your first impressions mean the world to me and I am always grateful for you!

Kickstarter backers - your support means the world to me! Thank you!

And finally, my family. None of this could happen without your support, love, and encouragement! Thank you so much!

Portrait by Three Ravens Art

Natalie Jess is a Midwest author who loves living in a place with snowy winters. She grew up reading way past her bedtime and never broke that habit - except now the books she reads, and writes, are definitely for adults.

Learn more at https://www.natalieandevy.com/